POTIONS AND PROSECCO

MERRY MEET COZY WITCH MYSTERIES: BOOK 2

LUNA MARTIN

JACWILLOW PRESS

For my sister,
I hope my wish comes true ...

Not everything that lies in the shadows is dark. But when rogue witches start appearing, it is not only the cocktails that start turning sour.

Daisy Banks' feet have been in two worlds long enough. And when a new friendship brings her to a prohibition themed night on a paddle steamer, she puts her best foot forward convinced that not every party in Folly Gate ends in murder ... right? But not everything is running smoothly in her new world ... Jasper is missing, and the follies are crumbling under her guard.

Following a hunch, she is determined to prove she deserves the trust of the local constabulary. But as she uncovers leads, someone in town is playing around with crossover potions – and the Grand Coven is demanding answers from her too.

Can Daisy balance her new life in Folly Gate and the demands of leading a coven? Or will it all be taken from her, extinguishing the Banks line forever?

A JACWILLOW PRESS Paperback

First Published in Great Britain in 2023 by JACWillow Press.

Paperback first published in 2023 by JACWillow Press

This paperback published in 2023 by JACWillow Press

Copyright © JACWillow Press 2023

Formatting by A. Martin

ISBN-13: 979-8852792983

Edited by A. Martin

Cover by Kim's Cozy Covers

CONTENTS

CHAPTER ONE

A LCHEMISTS ARE NOT YOUR friends – and that comes straight from
the High Coven. Jasper had told me that accepting Morton's help to
understand the Prime Spell Book could land me in more trouble than an-
ticipated. But I took the chance, even though I had heard about alchemists'
tools attracting witches. And I expect that what stood before me was only
the beginning. I remained seated in my aunt's reading chair, with Jasper by
my side. The crackling of wood in the roaring fireplace of the library: the
only sound breaking the silence. A rogue witch, Lucinda, stood in front of
us, her wand pointed directly at me.

"I know you have it," she said. "Which one is it?"

"I don't think it would be wise to start anything here," I said. "Without
a coven behind you, things might not end as well as you would like."

She held her gaze on me. "I don't need a coven," she said. "Why would
I want to answer to anyone? I can take what I want, when I want it. And
today I'll start with that Prime Spell Book you're hiding in here."

"I don't know what you *think* you are talking about," I said. My hand
twitched, waiting for my wand to snap, but it lay snug in my sleeve.

"Hold your ground," Jasper said. "She's a low-level witch. She can't do
much harm."

The witch let out a deep cackle and flicked her wand. "Then I'll find
it myself!" The force of her wand blew out my hair and then filled the

room with a quiet 'pop', no louder than the sound one would make when popping a finger on the inside of their cheek. A smoky orb appeared in front of her, illuminating the room in a dull green light.

I slowly rose from my chair – silently, my hands tucked loosely in my skirt pockets. "What is it, Jasper?" I asked him.

He arched his back and pricked his ears; his golden eyes began to follow the orb.

Lucinda chuckled. "Cats distract easily ..." she said. "And it seems your *familiar* is no different."

I tried to get his attention, "Jasper ... Jasper ... come here ..."

But it fixated him. The tiny ball of light started darting across the shelves, back and forth, scanning the rows of books in my aunt's library.

"I've heard rumours about you, Daisy," Lucinda snarled. "And it looks like they might be true." The solitary witch looked down and checked her nails, as if she found herself in similar situations more often than not. "They told me you didn't know what you were doing. A new witch" – she huffed – "in charge of her own coven? The rumours are growing, Daisy. And we know you have a Prime Spell Book. If it's not me that finds it, you will soon be fighting off a lot worse than me."

"I know nothing about a Prime Spell Book," I lied. "But if I hear anything, I'll let you know."

Lucinda tutted. "I've heard the same lie from your aunt," she said. "I'm not about to be fooled by an untrained witch like you."

The room was almost silent, apart from the low humming of the orb. Jasper watched it, still transfixed. The witch took her eyes off me for a few brief seconds to follow her orb. I waited. And the next time she moved her eyes, I seized my moment and threw the bottle I had been clutching in my skirt pocket. It smashed in front of Jasper, emitting a gigantic cloud of blue dust covering him in an instant. As the smoke cleared, I looked back at Lucinda. "I told you, working alone is not always the best decision for a witch."

She looked back at Jasper. His enormous paws prowled across the wooden floors, heading straight for Lucinda. His growl enveloped the room.

"He's a shifter?" Lucinda's face paled.

I didn't hide the sarcasm in my voice, "My aunt didn't tell you that either? I suggest you leave, Lucinda. And take your orb with you. It won't find anything here."

"There'll be more like me coming, Daisy. And they won't be so easy to dismiss. I can guarantee you that. If I can get in here—"

"Get out!" I demanded. My wand flicked from my sleeve and pointed in her direction, blowing a gush of wind that pinned her to the wall. "Leave!"

The force subsided, and she took a moment to straighten herself before huffing and puffing her way out of the library and through the opened French doors to my garden. As the doors closed hard behind her, we heard another quiet 'pop', as the green orb dissolved into thin air.

"You made nice work of her," Jasper said and returned to his usual feline form. "I'm impressed."

I picked him up and scratched his chest. "How do you think she got in here?" I asked him.

"Well, Edlynn has been telling you to upgrade your aunt's locks for a while now. I don't know why you haven't sorted it out sooner. But I'd re-charm them as quick as I could if I were you. Lucinda is only a low-level witch, and she got through them. If the rumours are growing, there's no reason there won't be higher-level witches looking to get their hands on whatever they think you aunt has left unattended. The Prime Spell Book might keep itself hidden from seeking orbs, but we don't know what else might be waiting for us." Jasper adjusted himself in my arms, which was his way of telling me he wanted to be put on the floor. I placed him down and he lifted his head in the air. "I have to say, Daisy, I feel clear-headed." He drew in a long breath. "In fact, I feel totally revitalised. Maybe I've missed guarding my witch more than I care to admit."

I reached down and scratched him behind the ears. "That's the clarity potion speaking," I said. "I left it in my pocket after my last class with Ailsa. You're only supposed to use a few drops. She's already quite unimpressed with my focus in her potion lessons, and I don't think using a whole bottle at once is going to get me any gold stars. You might feel like that for a while, at least for a few hours. Sorry, but it was the only way I had to get you to snap out of your trance with Lucinda's orb."

"Oh, no need to apologise." He lifted his paw to clean his cheek. "You'll get no complaints from me. I know Banks witches always have my best interests at heart."

"Although, I have to say, Jasper, it is a little worrying if all it takes to distract you is a little green light. We might have to work on something so it doesn't happen again."

"Well, your clarity potion did the trick. Unfortunately, it's a weakness with cat familiars. We have" – he drew in a breath – "*issues* ... with balls of light."

"We'll find something for you, Jasper. I'm sure of it." I patted him reassuringly and slumped back into my aunt's reading chair. Jasper, once again, took his place by my feet. "We're going to upgrade security," I said. I leant forward, rested on my elbows and looked at the portrait of my aunt above the warming fire. "How did she do it? So many secrets."

"She had a gift, Daisy. She would know there was trouble on the way a long time before it arrived. Although, it is sad to say, there were still times that caught her unaware. Especially the night we lost her. We had no warning, not even an inkling. All the training in the world wouldn't have helped her that night." He looked up at her portrait. "Rest in the shadows, Olivia."

I gave him a sympathetic smile. "She kept the Prime Spell Book safe. And I've already nearly lost it to a gossiping witch. Maybe I should just give it over to someone who knows more about guarding spell books."

"I've seen this before, Daisy. You think you can't do something when you can. You only need the right training and preparation to be ready. When you're prepared, these doubts will disappear ... *like magic*." He chuckled. "I promise. And if it's any consolation, I had to have the same conversation with your great-great grandmother. She didn't think she had any power in her at all. But we spent years fighting the dark alchemists. And we were quite a force together."

"Alchemists ... that's what's got us into this mess to start with." I picked up the magnifying glass Morton had given me. "It's broken now, anyway."

Jasper looked up at me. "An alchemist's looking glass might be helpful with maps, but they are no match for magic ... especially Prime Spells."

"Well, how was I supposed to know that? I thought it would help."

"You weren't supposed to know that ... but you do now. Remember, a witch knows what she needs to know when she needs to know it. But it might be best to stay away from alchemists' tools until you know for sure if you should use them. Keep a record of it, in your own grimoire. Your aunt gave you the release spell for her journal so you could learn from the Banks witches before you. Maybe now it's time you made your first journal entry – for the Banks witches that will come after you. There is a lot to learn, Daisy, but for today you have learned to protect the Prime Spell Book."

Frantic honking of a car horn interrupted our conversation. The pendulum chimed on the tall oak grandfather clock. "Ailsa," I said. "I better go, Jasper. You know what she's like when you're late."

Chapter Two

I slid on my boots and grabbed a raspberry muffin from the cake stand in my kitchen. "I won't be long," I said to Jasper. Ailsa waved out of the window of her car as I pulled back the curtain.

Her voice carried through the open front door, "Come on, Daisy. Don't dillydally. I said 10.00am sharp."

After smirking at Jasper, I headed out the door. "I'm coming ... What's the rush?" I asked as I opened the car door.

"The gates open at 10.30. I want to be the first in line," she replied.

"I don't know how much of a queue you are expecting at the gardens," I said.

"It might surprise you," Ailsa replied as she reversed out of the drive and onto the road, leaving the large gate to close behind us.

Mrs James, my not-so-friendly neighbour, was returning home from her morning walk with her small West Highland White Terrier. I raised a friendly hand to greet her. She paused for a moment, chose not to return my greeting and continued walking home.

"Don't worry about her," Edlynn said from the passenger front seat. "She wasn't your aunt's biggest fan either." She looked back at me and shrugged her shoulders. "We can't please everyone all the time."

It was a short drive to the gardens, but it gave me enough time to tell them about Lucinda.

"We may have to take these rumours a little more seriously," Edlynn said.

"It might be a good thing that she turned up," Ailsa added as she parked the car. "It gives you some time to prepare."

I slung my bag over my shoulder and closed the car door. "Prepare for what?" I asked. But Ailsa was already on her way to the gates. We were five minutes early ... *but,* much to her delight, she was the first in line.

I followed behind Ailsa with Edlynn. "Ailsa doesn't get excited about much," she said. "But when she does ... nothing will stand in her way."

Ailsa stood at the ticket window looking particularly pleased with herself, and even more pleased when the window slipped back and she was told she could go through the gates a few minutes early. She led the way down a narrow pebble path before arriving at a hard stop. "There it is," she said. "Isn't it magnificent?"

The magnolia tree stood tall, with its branches in full bloom. Its soft pink petals, with their champagne-like fragrance, wafted across us against the backdrop of a trickling stream.

"I told you it was the biggest in Britain," Ailsa said. "Not the tallest, but by far the widest. And it's not always in bloom when the gardens first open. We are the first to see it this year."

Edlynn took a step back, hung her basket over her elbow and admired the giant tree. "Definitely worth the drive, Ailsa," she said.

"And you see that stream there, Daisy? It has a waterfall around the corner. We'll walk up there in a minute. But the stream flows all the way down to the cathedral in Lowes End, where it's cornered at the well. It is supposed to have healing properties. Apparently, they used to take children there to cure them of whooping cough and rickets. I don't know about nowadays, as it has a less than holistic journey right down to a cattle trough. Most good witches know you can find water blessed by the pixies down there after the winter solstice. You have to be quick enough to draw the first cup, though. It's quite sought-after for filling shelves of potion rooms." Ailsa looked up from her brochure. "What do you think, Daisy? Your aunt loved it here."

"It's beautiful," I said with a smile. "Let me get a picture of you both." I held up my camera and moved the dial to the manual settings. They hadn't changed since I took a photography class five years ago.

Ailsa stood as proud as the magnolia tree with her arm around her friend's shoulder and a wide smile across her face. "In a few weeks, those woods will fill with bluebells," she said. "We'll have to come back. You'll get some topnotch pictures then."

"Maybe I will," I said.

We continued along the winding path and across an old stone bridge until we reached the end of the path. The scattered waterfalls fell into a large pond before cascading off to meet the stream.

"Let's sit down here," Ailsa said. "We can take in the view."

We walked towards the well-manicured picnic area. The freshly painted wooden bench left a small brass plaque exposed. It read: 'For Charlie, until we walk together again, Jane, 1988.' I wondered if Jane was walking with him again yet as I placed my bag down and took a seat.

Edlynn stood up with her basket and passed us both a napkin. "What would you like for morning tea?"

"Well, Lucinda interrupted my breakfast this morning ..." I said.

"How about a nice scotch egg then?"

"I'll take one too," Ailsa said.

Edlynn lifted the side of her basket and pulled out an elegant pair of vintage tongs. "One for you, Daisy ... and Ailsa." She sat down on the bench and pulled herself out a slice of bakewell tart. "There's plenty more if you want some." She took a bite of her morning tea. "I think you were fortunate with Lucinda, Daisy. It has to be a priority to get those locks re-charmed. Maybe we should get started on them when we get back today. Ailsa has been working on something for you."

"It's an old recipe ... but a good one," Ailsa said. "It will have to do until you can find something better."

"Thanks," I said. "I don't think it will take long to find what we need. My wand has been throwing study scrolls at me, left, right and centre ... and sometimes quite literally."

Edlynn giggled. "I told you. You have quite the ambitious wand there. We'll finish our tea and head back to your house."

"Okay," I said as I took another bite.

Edlynn pulled a thermos from her basket and made tea.

"I have some news," I said. "Cara phoned last night and told me her Estate Agent has found a buyer for my flat in London."

Edlynn's eyes widened. "*And* ...?"

"I've accepted the offer," I said.

Ailsa smiled. "That sold quickly."

"I know. That's why I thought I should accept. I might have caught a lucky break."

"Oh, it's never luck," Edlynn said. "Everything has an order, remember?"

I smiled at my friends. "I've had time to think since I've been in Folly Gate and ... the truth of it is ... I think I have been holding onto a life that is no longer there. After Dad died ... and my friends ... well, they all have their own lives to live. The flat was quite empty on my own. And Cara ... well, she is rarely in London anymore. I wrapped my whole life around—"

"You don't have to explain," Edlynn said. "I'm happy to hear Cara will be visiting. *Some* childhood friendships are bound never to end. And we couldn't be happier that you have made Folly Gate home. It always *was* home, anyway. But your father did his best to protect you from a world he knew little about. And your aunt Olivia did her best to respect that decision. We missed you when you left, though ... *terribly*."

We sat for a while, listening to the sounds of the birds and the water and the murmured conversations of visitors to the garden. "I think it's best we head back," Ailsa suggested. "We need to attend to your locks. The sooner they're fixed, the better."

"I agree," Edlynn said as she closed her basket.

We stopped briefly at the nursery on our way out, purchasing some potted plants to take home for our own gardens. Edlynn chatted about how much I will love my new life in Folly Gate, and we headed to the car and started off on the winding road back to Folly Gate. I looked out the window and pondered my decision as we passed a dead badger that lay bloodied on the side of the road.

"Poor thing," I said out aloud. "It's so sad when they cull them."

"It's survival of the fittest, unfortunately sometimes," Ailsa said as she adjusted her rear-view mirror.

As we turned a hairpin corner, we came across a figure standing at the side of a 4 wheel-drive, the back open and a tyre leaning on its side.

"Is that Kate?" Edlynn asked.

"It could be ..." Ailsa said as she slowed to the edge of the road.

Edlynn opened her door and walked over to the woman, greeting her friend with a hug. Ailsa released her seatbelt, and I followed suit. "We thought that was you," Ailsa said as she closed her door.

"*Flat tyre* ... as you can see," she said.

Edlynn took care of the introductions. "Daisy, this is Kate. She has the wildlife hospital on the outskirts of town."

"Nice to meet you," Kate said. "It's hedgehogs today. I think we found a courting couple, but the female wasn't doing well, so I took her to the vet for some x-rays." She looked across at me. "Have you ever seen a hedgehog getting an x-ray?" she asked.

"Um, I can't say that I have," I replied.

"You should look it up if you want a giggle. I still have little Jack with me. Do you want to see him? He's adorable."

"Sure, why not," I said as I followed her swishing ponytail to the hedge side of her car.

"Just lift the towel back," she said. "He might be snuggled up in there."

I peered into the car. "Oh, you're right," I said. "He *is* adorable."

"Let me give you a better look at him," Kate said. She scooped him up out of his box and proceeded to fill me in on all the hedgehog facts she could think of at the time, showing me his little feet and cute little nose as it sniffed the air.

"Oh, he has a stick stuck on his tummy," I said.

"That's not a *stick* ..." She stifled a giggle.

"Oh, I do beg your pardon, Jack," I said.

Edlynn's voice came from the back of the car, "All done, Kate!"

Kate placed the hedgehog back in its box and walked to Edlynn. "You fixed my tyre? I didn't know you were—"

"It's no problem. It's something that was taught to me one day and I've never forgotten."

"Well, thank you," she said, looking a little confused. "Well ... how can I repay you?"

"Oh, there's no need for that," Edlynn said.

"Well, I would like to. Who knows how long I might have been stuck here?" She took a moment to think. "I know. How about a party? I'm having a party, for my 30th, and I could easily make space for three more. We are taking a paddle steamer down the River Dart. There will be a buffet and dancing—"

"Dancing?" Edlynn interrupted. "Well, I've never been one to say no to a dance."

"You'll come then?" Kate asked.

"We'd love to go," Edlynn replied.

"Perfect! Well, we are taking the Southern Angel steam train at 5:17pm. It will take us there and I have a bus to bring us back to The Cidered Apple. It will be a lot of fun. I guarantee it."

"I'm sure it will," Ailsa said.

"Well, thank you again. I better get Jack home. I'll see you on Saturday."

We headed back to Ailsa's car, but before we could pull out, Kate dashed towards us, waving for us to wait. Ailsa wound down the window of her classic Triumph Herald.

Kate leant down into the window, a little breathless. "I almost forgot to tell you, it's a *themed* party."

"No problem," Edlynn said. "We love a good dress-up."

"Good," Kate said. "Then you'll love this one: 'Prohibition & Prosecco'. Flapper girls, smart suits, that sort of thing."

"Sounds like a lot of fun," I said. "And as it happens, I think I have the perfect gift."

CHAPTER THREE

WE ARRIVED HOME AFTER a short drive. Ailsa and Edlynn followed me around the back, carrying the plants we bought from the garden nursery: some poppies, strawberry plants, fresh basil and a mushroom kit.

Ailsa stood on the patio and surveyed my work. "The water lilies are looking beautiful, Daisy."

"Thanks," I said. "Every garden should have a pond ... if you can. I found the overgrown remnants of one and thought I would put it to use."

"It's good for the wildlife," Edlynn proclaimed.

"Indeed," Ailsa said, as proudly as if she had dug it herself.

"Maybe we could attract a sweet frog for you to kiss?" I teased Ailsa.

"My frog kissing days are long gone," she announced, with light-hearted disapproval. "Have you thought any more about where you might place a herb garden? There's a perfect spot in the back there, right near the gazebo. It will get the right amount of sun ... and you have a potting shed right next to it."

"I have started a design," I said. "Maybe you can have a look at it?"

"Of course. Whenever you're ready. But while we are all together, can we speak with you about something? We didn't get the chance at the gardens. Some places are best enjoyed in some peace and quiet."

"Oh, I'm intrigued. What is it?" I looked at Edlynn, a little confused.

"Well," Edlynn said. "It's nothing to worry about ... but we're a little concerned about you, that's all. And it's one of the reasons why we thought a nice drive to the gardens might do you good."

"Oh. How so?" I asked.

"Let's be honest, Daisy. You haven't really left the house except to go to the shop, for a few weeks now. And this is the first time we have seen you out of your jeans in ... I don't know how long. We just wanted to know everything is okay with you?"

"Yes, everything is okay ... and there's nothing wrong with a good pair of jeans ... they're comfortable. I don't think I need to look like a *fashionista* to go and pick up some milk and bread. Thank you for the concern, though. But there are only so many hours in a day, you know? And I really want to focus on my studies so that we can work more with the Prime Spell Book. Aunt Olivia left it to me for a reason. And the Banks witches have always been the guardians of it. I don't want to let anyone down, but I can only focus on so much ... and, as you can see, I've been spending quite a bit of time in the garden. I'm finding it rather meditative – getting my hands dirty and watching my work pay off. I'm surprised at how rewarding it is. But you have nothing to worry about. And, I promise, I'll make an effort for Kate's party. I've simply been taking some time to find my feet."

"Well, if that's all it is then ..." Ailsa smiled, and Edlynn gave me an understanding nod.

"And," I continued, "not to mention, with the Prime Spell Book opened and working, we could have an advantage ... a *bargaining tool*."

"A bargaining tool? For what?" Ailsa asked.

"Whatever comes up," I said. "For instance ... with Morton."

"I'd steer clear of him, Daisy," Ailsa said. "I know your aunt used to work with him on occasion, but we never knew what for ... or when."

"I'm going to meet him tomorrow," I said. "I'll keep you posted." I quickly changed the subject, "Anyway, I've got bigger problems on my hands at the moment. Come with me. I've got something to show you."

They eagerly followed me down to a corner of the garden. Ailsa carried the crate filled with my new plants. I turned, paused and looked at them both. "I agree with you, Ailsa. I think this spot would be perfect for a herb garden. However ..."

"What is it?" Ailsa asked, impatiently.

"Follow me." I flipped open the latch on the potting shed door. "Go through to the greenhouse ... you'll see. I have been trying Ailsa ... but look at my seedlings. I've done everything you taught me."

"Oh dear, Daisy." Ailsa looked around the greenhouse inspecting the small pots of fading rosemary, thyme and mint. "This isn't good. I don't know how you've managed it ... but every pot?"

"I know. I have no idea what I did wrong. But look at them – the poor things. Every single one of them ... dead!"

Ailsa looked impressed with my enthusiasm, but not so much with the state of my greenhouse. "Don't worry, Daisy," she said. "I've got something that will bring these little darlings back to life. A witch's greenhouse doesn't need to look like this. And at least we have something to work with, I suppose."

I looped my arm through Ailsa's and rested my head on her shoulder. "Thank you, Ailsa. I had hoped you might help," I said. "And now that I can release my green-thumb shame, let's get inside and I'll put the kettle on."

We placed our newly acquired plants on the potting table and headed back towards the house. I unlocked the back French doors, and as I walked into the sitting room, I saw a woman stirring on my sofa. When her opening eyes caught us, she sat straight up and froze.

The three of us went to snap our wands when a familiar voice came from my aunt's library, "Merry Meet, Daisy. It's okay. She's with me."

"Scarlet?"

"Yes." She stepped forward to greet us. "Sorry to arrive unannounced. But we thought it necessary. Amber," – she gestured at her friend – "this is Daisy, Ailsa and Edlynn."

The stranger stood up and smiled feebly, her hair matted and sticking out from the left side of her head. Scarlet motioned at her hair.

"Oh," she said and smoothed her palms down her topaz hair until it sat perfectly framed around her face. She looked across at Scarlet then back at me. "You were right. She looks exactly like her."

I looked at Amber suspiciously, still trying to figure out what would call for a visit from two shadow witches.

"We came to help," Scarlet said. "The rumours are swirling and we thought there might be trouble. When we arrived here, the back doors were open and we decided to stay until you got home."

"I'm sure I locked them before we left for the gardens," I said. "And where's Jasper?"

Scarlet moved into the sitting room. "Nowhere to be seen ... and we've been here a few hours. Amber was keeping an eye on the back door. And when we saw the smashed potion bottle on the floor, we knew something must have happened."

"You're right," I said. "Something did happen. I had a visit from a low-level witch, looking for a Prime Spell Book."

Scarlet paused for a moment and looked me directly in the eye. "We know you have it," she said.

I snapped my wand, and Ailsa and Edlynn followed suit. The three of us poised to strike at any moment.

"There's no need for that," Scarlet said, holding up her two wand-free hands. "Let me be clear: we have never seen it, but we knew your aunt had one."

"Why would you say that?" I asked, not taking my eyes off them.

"Because … because she told us …"

"She told you what?" I asked, unconvinced of their intentions.

Scarlet reached into a pocket of her long-layered skirt and pulled out a scroll. "Because, Daisy, we have pages from it." She passed me the scroll and motioned to Amber who followed her lead, reaching into her deep pockets and passing me another scroll.

I retracted my wand, but Ailsa and Edlynn were still not as trusting. I opened the first scroll. "It's blank."

"For now …" Scarlet said. "But open Amber's scroll."

As I unrolled the second scroll, they both lifted from my hands. And as the pages floated mid-air, they started to stitch themselves together, before returning to my open hands. "The missing pages?" I asked, in a hushed tone.

"Well, two of them …" Scarlet replied. "But there are more … hidden amongst other shadow witches."

"Follow me," I said and motioned for Ailsa and Edlynn to lower their wands. I stood in front of the bookshelf and turned to see the four women standing in front of me. Their expressions were solemn as if they knew this was going to happen. They didn't move, but a softness swept over their faces. I reached up for the Prime Spell Book, hidden in plain sight under the title of *The Amused Muse*. I hadn't seen that title before, but the book and its black leather binding made it instantly recognisable. It slowly drifted from the shelf falling gently into my hands. I took it over to my aunt's reading chair and sat down, opened its pages, and held the stitched pages from Scarlet and Amber above it. The large grimoire's pages began flicking until they stopped about three quarters of the way through. The two pages slipped out of my hands, and in a covering of silver dust, they wriggled their way snug into their rightful place. My wand snapped from my sleeve, as if it responded to a call to work, and began furiously moving over the open pages, just as it had done before – the only difference being that when it had happened before, Jasper had been by my side. We stood in silence, watching my wand finish its work, before laying itself on the page for a moment, as if to rest, and slowly finding its way back into my sleeve.

"What does it say?" Edlynn's voice whispered across the room.

"More spells," I said. "New spells, I guess." I looked up to see Amber's awe-struck eyes. Scarlet, Edlynn and Ailsa looked more curious, like it wasn't so unusual for them. "Spells ... for *protection*, I think."

Edlynn stepped towards me. "Well, a witch knows what she needs to know when she needs to know it. It sounds like it's time to secure this house. We can't have just anyone walking in here trying to get their hands on the Prime Spell Book."

"Didn't you say you had something we could use, Ailsa?" I asked.

She answered with a dignified "Yes," then continued, "But I also said I had something you could use until you found something better. I couldn't offer anything stronger than what the Prime Spell Book can offer."

I looked down at the open page of the book. "*Locks and Laces ...*"

"That will be it," Ailsa said. "It makes perfect sense. There's nothing worse than a *one-booted* witch. And loose laces will send your broom plummeting straight to the ground."

"*Scarlet ... Amber ...*" I said. "Thank you for the pages." They dipped their heads politely. "But why didn't you bring them to me earlier?"

"I tried," Scarlet replied. "But when I first met you, after you called me on your aunt's phone, you told me you weren't yet assigned to your magic. And then when Amber received a jumbled memory orb—"

"A what?" I asked.

Scarlet answered without hesitation, "It's a little difficult to explain, but the simple version is that shadow witches can create small balls of energy ... that when used correctly can store information ... notes, recipes, spells ... reminders, that sort of thing. But they can usually only be used while the witch is alive. Under normal circumstances, all that stored energy would go to the witch's grave ... where it's needed ... for crossing over. When it's time you can collect them up and use them to make the journey ... easier. They're very useful for hiding anything you wouldn't want found."

"*Like* ... a Prime Spell Book," Amber said.

"I'm not following," I said. "Are you saying Aunt Olivia is alive?"

Scarlet clasped her hands together in thought. "Under normal circumstances, I would say Olivia would have to be alive. But we were all at her funeral. We saw her. She had crossed."

"When did she give you these pages?" I asked.

"Only a few weeks before she crossed." Scarlet paced the floor. "It's like she knew something was going to happen. When she gave me the page, she said I would know when to use it. But that's all she told me, apart from it being from the Prime Spell Book. It was almost as if she was trying to protect herself from something. I mean, why didn't she keep them in memory orbs and take them to the shadows with her?"

"Maybe she didn't want them to go with her ... to the grave," I said. "And you're right. It doesn't make sense. Your pages did reveal the *Locks and Laces* spell, though. We have to find the other pages. Amber, what about you? Did Aunt Olivia say anything else when you saw her?"

"No. Only that I would know when it was time to use it. And when Scarlet first came to visit me about them, we agreed it wasn't time. That was until the memory orb ... It caught me unaware, in the dead of the night. I couldn't quite make it out, and when I saw it, all I could do was call for

Olivia. The confusion set in when I realised it couldn't be ... because she was dead. Sorry, Daisy."

"It's okay, Amber," I said. "I am as confused as you are. We didn't think anyone else knew about the Prime Spells, except for the three of us. Ailsa and Edlynn were her best friends, but she even managed to keep it hidden from them. She must have had her reasons to do that, though." I looked to my aunt's portrait above the mantelpiece. Nothing had changed there: she still held a posy of daisies. "We will have to find our own way out of this. My aunt is trying to tell us something, and if a witch knows what she needs to know when she needs to know it, then I think we should get started on the spells that have been given to us. We have to secure this house, especially this library. Even if we don't know why yet." I decided to delegate. "Ailsa, you check what herbs we need. Edlynn, you organise equipment. And Amber and Scarlet, you can help with any shadow items we might need." I lifted the spell book up onto the lectern, where I knew my aunt would have spent many days and nights studying in her library. "We will have to do the best we can to follow my aunt's lead."

But as the five of us crowded around discussing who should do what, I was still wondering why Jasper hadn't come home yet. And what ... or even *who* ... had made him leave so quickly ...

CHAPTER FOUR

I PEERED THROUGH THE dust covered windows of the potting shed, hoping Jasper might have followed us in after returning from the gardens. As I walked in, a piece of broken terracotta pot crunched against the rotting floorboards under my boot. I searched everywhere, from the high decrepit shelving to the low damp hidden corners of the shed, but I could find no trace of him. As I walked across the stone bridge to the fields, I called and scoured every nook and cranny I could find. But no Jasper ... and no help from my wand. I thought something might connect us, like when a twin or a close sibling can feel when you are in trouble ... but I couldn't feel anything ... nothing at all. I huffed and searched, trying to reassure myself by thinking he was on the prowl and would be home soon. But something didn't sit right with me ... and I could *feel* that.

I headed home to start working on the locks. Maybe by the time we finished the spell, I would find him curled up in front of the fire, and all the worrying would have been for nothing. As I walked back, I checked through hedges and a *ha-ha* designed to keep livestock safe. I hoped the moors of Devon would do the same for my Jasper.

The back door opened into a small granite floored boot room for removing muddy wellington boots and hanging soaking coats. Amber greeted me at the door, "We decided to start at the top ... if you're ready," her voice filled with a quiet excitement.

"I'll bring the spell book and meet you up there," I replied. As I walked through to the library, I hoped Jasper was all right ... wherever he was. My bare feet scurried across the wooden floor to the lectern where the Prime Spell Book lay open. But as I went to pick it up, something caught my eye: my aunt's portrait, with its blackened background, now pulsated with a copper light, changing back and forth from its darkness and then again back to light. I stopped for a moment and watched it. The room became icy cold, and I could hear slow dripping water. I recognised the sound but couldn't think where I had heard it. I reached up to the painting, but the sound stopped ... and the painting returned to its usual state.

"More secrets ..." I said aloud, before taking the spell book and heading up the stairs, where my newly formed alliance of friends waited for me.

"We're in here," I heard Ailsa's voice come from the empty room at the top of the stairs. I entered. The four witches stood around a silver tray, laden with collected ingredients needed for our *Locks and Laces* spell, including mugwort, pennyroyal, rose geranium and a little dragon's blood. Each witch held their wand in their hand, ready to begin.

"We thought it best to start in here," Edlynn said.

I readied my wand. "Why do you think it's called a *Locks and Laces* spell?" I asked.

"That's easy to answer," Ailsa began. "It is a protection spell in its own right ... but also more of a survival spell. You have two choices when in danger: you either stay and fight, or run in flight. Personally, I prefer to *fight*. I'd rather do anything than *flight* ... especially on something as unreliable as a broomstick."

"I see ..." I said.

Edlynn's excitement at spellcasting brought us back into focus. "Well, there's only one window in this room. Let's get started here." She looked at me. "What are the instructions?"

As I began to read the spell, our wands formed a visible force in the centre of our circle. We were a little clumsy at first, but with patience, we managed to hold the sphere at the tip of our wands and bring it down into the waiting potion bottle. When the vapour subsided, I picked up the delicate blue glass bottle, placed the dropper in the top and walked over to the window latch, carefully placing three drops of our freshly brewed potion onto its handle, and stepped back. The window let out a loud groan and creak before making a quiet locking sound, letting us know the charmed liquid had worked.

"That should do it," Ailsa said as she jiggled the lock to make sure. "As tight as my laces," she added. "Although you would still never catch me on a broom. Onto the next one, shall we? Two windows and one door, I think … off the top of my head."

Scarlet picked up the silver tray that lay resting on an old carved chest – I had no idea of its contents yet. My aunt had an obsession with collecting old chests and filling them with all manner of curiosities. Maybe she was a pirate in her past life and had found her way back home to Folly Gate.

We filed out behind Edlynn, wands in hand and ready to get the house and the Prime Spell Book as safe as we could. The smell of rose geranium incense followed Scarlet, and although we were quiet over the hours it took to secure the house, it was not an uncomfortable silence. We continued our ritual, passing over the windows and doors of each room of the top floor, before making our way up to the attic and swiftly working our way down the remaining two floors. The last lock to be charmed was the front door, which I had recently wiped over with peppermint oil and made sure my aunt's broomstick sat by it, snug on its hooks.

"Thank you," I said, as I closed the bottle for the last time.

Edlynn flicked her wand into her sleeve. "No bother at all, Daisy. Why don't you put the spell book away and I'll put on some rose petal tea?"

Scarlet followed me through to the library, carrying the silver tray. "Well, that should keep you and that book safe for a while," she said, as she placed the tray on my aunt's writing desk.

I raised my fingers to my lips. "Do you hear that?" I asked her.

"That dripping sound?" she replied.

"Yes, it's coming from the painting of Aunt Olivia."

Scarlet stepped closer to inspect the artwork. "Why is it glowing like that?"

"I think Aunt Olivia is trying to tell me something," I said. "But I have no idea what." I bit my bottom lip, trying hard to remember where I had heard the sound. And then it hit me, like a lightning bolt in a Folly Gate storm. "The follies!" I shouted. "Jasper must be in the follies!"

Scarlet looked confused. "But why would he ... *without you?*"

I ran to the boot room with Scarlet in tow. "You'll have to let yourself out ... or stay ... I don't mind," I said as I grabbed my cloak and shoved my feet into my boots.

The others had heard the kerfuffle, and Edlynn reached out to help me put on my cloak. "What is it, Daisy?" she asked.

I turned for a moment to be met with concerned faces. I suppose after their generous offer to help secure the house, abandoning them might not be considered the most hospitable of actions. "It's Jasper," I said. "I think I know where he is."

Ailsa reached for her coat. "Well, we'll come with you."

"You can't," I said. "I can't cross you all over into the follies. He's in there. I'm sure of it. I'll have to explain later."

"But how is he in the follies without you?" Edlynn asked.

I buttoned my cloak. "That's what I have to find out. I'm sorry. I have to go."

"Of course," Scarlet said. "Go ... Merry Pass."

I nodded. "Merry Meet again," I replied.

The back door opened. "The potion must have worked," I said. "I'll let you know when I find him." I took one step out and was stopped in my boots by an almighty crash, followed by a loud moan coming from deep within the back garden. "What was that?" I asked as I peered out into the darkness.

Without hesitation, we all flicked our wands from our sleeves and charged directly towards the sound. What greeted us was a little unexpected – to say the least. Two striped stockinged legs hung precariously from the large *gazebo-shading* Rowan tree. A broomstick, snapped in half, balanced on one of the larger branches. Whoever it was, their skirt had fallen all the way up and over their shoulders, and covered their face. As we moved in closer, we could see two flailing arms trying, without success, to remove the long skirt from their face. A small grey mouse ran quickly up the stockinged legs and perched itself right on the tip of her boot; his little hands clasped together and his nose twitching furiously.

"Ugh," Ailsa declared. "Put your wands away. She's old school."

"Old school? How can you tell?" I asked in a whispered tone.

"Look at the britches on her ..." she said.

I looked back at the hanging woman's lacy knee-length undershorts. "Ohhh ... I see ... the *britches*."

Scarlet stepped forward and helped to remove the skirt from the woman's face. "Em?"

"Olivia? Is that you? Get me down from here," she demanded.

"That's what you get for wearing loose laces," Ailsa said smugly.

Edlynn picked up the small mouse, and we helped to remove the faltered witch from the tree. Once down, she took back her mouse, who scurried his way back into the top pocket of her velvet green blazer.

"Here," Scarlet said and passed her a pair of fallen spectacles. "What are you doing here, Em?"

She looked around, inspecting us as she tried to regain her composure. "I suspect ..." she said, as she brushed off her skirt, "... the same thing as you, Scarlet. Olivia! Where is she?"

Chapter Five

I had to wonder how many more witches would find their way into my house. I hoped the *Locks and Laces* spell would hold ... but my aunt Olivia had a lot of explaining to do. And until I could figure out why so many witches were turning up unannounced, I had to bring my focus back to Jasper. I stood with one *booted* foot in my sitting room doorway and the other ready to leave. The now five witches sat with rose petal teas in hand, listening intently to our latest arrival.

"I was sure I was going to find Olivia here," Em said. "A witch like her doesn't simply vanish into the shadows. The scroll from her appeared next to my bed this morning. I have no idea what it means, but I had heard Daisy moved to Folly Gate and thought she might have a clue. Do any of you know why Olivia is leaving us all messages?"

Em passed me the scroll. "No ... we don't. Not yet anyway. I'm trying to figure it out, but right now there are bigger problems: Jasper is missing. All of this is going to have to wait. I am going to look for him."

"Oh, Jasper is still here?" Em asked. "Well, I suppose he's always been with the Banks witches. It makes perfect sense for the High Coven to assign him to you. Olivia would be pleased, I'm sure." She sipped on her tea. "Where do you think he is?"

"He's usually home by now, but I have a suspicion he might be in the follies. I don't have time to explain, but I need to get there as soon as I can. I was on my way there when you ... *arrived*."

Em stood up from her chair. "I don't know if it's a good idea for such a young witch to be messing around with follies."

Ailsa chuckled. "I agree. And the more I get to know you, Em, the more I like you."

Em looked across at me. "I don't know what all the fuss is about with the follies. They should have remained sealed. And whatever was found crawling around should have been shut tight in there, too. The High Covens have never known what could be running around in them. They should have been left as a wealthy man's eccentricity. Secret passages hidden behind miniature garden buildings," she scoffed. "Who knows where you could end up? For all we know, you could walk into a folly and step out into the middle of the Egyptian Pyramids. Nobody knows ... *including* the Banks witches."

Ailsa nodded her head. "I couldn't agree more. Nothing good ever seems to come out of those follies."

I defended my aunt's work, "I would think they were a good way to travel. We moved 15 miles from the Folly Gate entrance all the way down to the coast in a few short minutes."

"I understand that," Em said. "And I suppose that could give us an advantage. But they've never been properly mapped. And we don't know what they do, even with your family investigating them for centuries. Not even the alchemists know. Although, if they did, it would be unlikely they would tell us."

I reached down and secured my boots. "Well, we're going to have to discuss this later. I need to get to the folly."

Em stepped closer to me. "You're going into the follies ... *alone?*"

"Yes, well, I don't have a choice," I replied. "Like I said, I can't cross Edlynn and Ailsa over and keep everyone in the follies at the same time."

"These young shadow witches." Em sighed, before looking across at Scarlet and Amber. "You didn't tell her?"

"A witch knows what she needs to know when she needs to know it," Scarlet replied.

"I understand all that nonsense," Em said. "But I think it is only fair Daisy knows that *all shadows* can move through the follies. However ... they need permission." Scarlet raised an eyebrow and Em continued, "Maybe *that* is something Daisy *needs* to know."

"I never knew ..." Edlynn shrugged.

"Well, thank you, Em," I said. "And where would we get this *permission* from?"

Amber tussled her hair casually. "That permission could come from you, Daisy. Under normal circumstances, it would have to come from the High Coven. But the Banks witches have always had access to the follies ..."

"Good. Then that makes it easy. You *all* have my permission. Let's go and we can discuss anything else on the way." I gestured with my hands to hurry them out of the room.

Ailsa picked up her tea. "Merry Pass," she said and bit into one of her homemade custard cream biscuits.

Edlynn stepped next to Ailsa. "Yes, Merry Pass," she said. "We'll stay here in case Jasper returns."

I paused for a moment, understanding Ailsa's aversion to follies and Edlynn's desire to stand with her friend. I could only hope that in the future we would smooth over the divide between *shadows* and other witches. But for now, we had to find Jasper.

Edlynn smiled gently.

I passed Em's scroll to Edlynn. "Merry Meet again," I said and tossed my swing bag over my shoulder.

The four of us left Ailsa and Edlynn at the house and made our way through the large wrought iron front gate. Mrs James, my not-so-friendly neighbour, stepped out of her MINI Cooper and turned in our direction. From the look on her face as it caught under the lamplight, we were quite the sight.

I looked back across at her as we scurried along the footpath. "Friends from London ..." I waved from across the street. "They're visiting for a few days."

Mrs James didn't move an inch, but I felt her stony stare on my back before turning down the avenue, out of sight.

Our boots and long skirts shuffled through the dimly lit cobbled streets and alleyways, as we took the quickest route down the 77 steps and on to the Yew tree in Folly Gate Field.

"We all know what to do?" I asked when we arrived.

The three shadow witches nodded in unison and we began circling the Yew tree ... once ... twice ... and thrice, *leaving the world behind ... no longer there*. We stepped into the deserted Folly Gate Fair and headed straight for the folly entrance. I felt possessed, like I knew exactly what I was doing, when in reality I had no idea what I was doing at all. But the three shadows behind me followed as if they believed I did. Maybe the portrait of my aunt had nothing to do with Jasper, but something kept my feet moving, one foot in front of the other.

When we arrived at the entrance, we placed our hands on the granite rock, closed our eyes, and when we opened them, we were standing in the heart of the cave system. I thought of Jasper and the first time he showed me he was a shifter: we were standing in this very spot.

My wand flicked from my sleeve, illuminating the cave, as it had done before. The only difference: Jasper had been by my side, not three shadow witches.

"Which way?" Amber's voice came from behind me.

My wand pointed towards the second entrance from the right. Jasper and I had been in there before, but had found nothing but a dead end. We followed my wand's lead, deep into the cavern, and I heard the familiar sounds of the dripping stalactites. "He has to be in here somewhere," I said.

"Don't worry," Scarlet reassured me. "We'll find him."

"Could be anywhere in here," Em said as she cast her wand forward to direct more light.

I scoured the cave walls, looking for anywhere Jasper might hide. After a short distance we came to a stop. "The cave wasn't like this," I said. "The end was further down. It looks like it has collapsed."

"These follies have a mind of their own," Em said. "That's what makes them so hard to map. You think you have it and then they change. It's an impossible task your family agreed to all those centuries ago."

My wand insisted on moving forward, slipping out of my hand and hovering to light the blockage. We moved a few of the smaller rocks out of the way when I heard a familiar growl. "Jasper? Jasper! Is that you?"

"Daisy …" he replied.

"What are you doing in here?" I asked him as we began frantically moving more of the broken rocks. "Are you okay? Are you hurt?"

"I'm not hurt … but I am trapped. Get me out of here."

"We're doing our best," I said, catching my breath.

"*We?*" He growled back.

"What happened?" I looked through a small opening but could see nothing in the darkness.

"A cauldron of bats," he said. "They flew through the cave and the vibration set off a collapse. But that's the least of our worries."

"Oh, Jasper," I said desperately. "I see you. Come this way."

I reached through the small hole and felt his cold fur as he shifted into his usual feline self. Dust-covered and tired, I pulled him through the small space and close into my chest.

"Here, give me your hand." Scarlet poured some water from a flask into my cupped hand for Jasper.

"You better tell me what's going on, Jasper," I said, as he lapped up as much water as he could.

"It's Gwendolyn," he replied. "And a crossover potion ... the potion the bats stole from me."

"Gwendolyn? And what do you mean '*bats stole from you*'?"

Scarlet, Amber and Em huddled forward together, hoping I would let them in on the conversation ... but they knew better than to ask.

"I think we better get out of here first," Jasper said. "But it seems someone else has access to the follies ... *without permission* ... and Gwendolyn doesn't know who. I went in to search the caves and see what or who I could find. But the bats ... they came out of nowhere and by the time I had fought them off, I realised the potion had been taken. If you hadn't arrived ... well, I'd rather not think about it. I'm already eight lives down."

"Why didn't Gwendolyn ask me to go with you? I could have moved through the follies. And I wouldn't have needed any potions."

"Gwendolyn doesn't exactly know I'm here. She came looking for you, and when I overheard her speaking to the Grand Coven Messenger, I came straight to the folly. Nobody knows who has been causing the destruction in the follies. But it seems like it is spreading. It could be anyone ... and Gwendolyn has been ordered to make sure it is no one in the Southern Covens. I got straight to work – to prove it's not you."

"Me? Why would I be going around destroying the follies all willy nilly? What would be the point of that? I barely know what they do."

"I know that, Daisy. You don't have to convince me. But Gwendolyn ... even though she is a High Priestess, she still has to answer to the Grand Coven. And unfortunately, for you ... you're their prime suspect!"

CHAPTER SIX

T HE THREE WITCHES FUSSED over Jasper for a moment before we made our way towards to the cave's entrance. Jasper pressed his cheek into their palms and greeted his old friends.

"Olivia would be so pleased to know you are with Daisy," Em said as she stood up. "We'll lead the way out," she offered. "I think you and Jasper have some catching up to do."

Jasper agreed with a purr.

The dark and damp cave lit up with the glowing lights from their wands.

"Why would I be at the top of the Grand Coven's suspect list?" I asked Jasper, as we followed them.

"The Messenger said you're the only one in Gwendolyn's coven that has access to the follies without the need for permission. And your *follysight* is getting stronger. You've opened so many follies in such a short time. It would be fickle of them not to consider you."

"So, she uses my familiar to get the information she wants?"

"No. She doesn't know I came here. My loyalty is always to my witch. When I overheard her speaking with the Messenger, I knew the time had come to continue Olivia's work. May she rest in the shadows."

Amber turned back and shone her wand on the ground. "Watch your step."

Jasper continued, "Your aunt had been working on a new crossover potion. I knew it worked because we had tested it. Olivia believed all shadows should have access to the follies ... *without permission.* She knew the Grand Coven would never agree, so she kept her work secret. There are others that have tried to make the potion ... and have failed. Although a pretty penny is made by traders for counterfeits, often sold as trinkets and souvenirs."

"But now that potion is missing," I said.

"I know. And I also know you are not the one damaging the follies. We have nothing to hide. But it is Gwendolyn's priority to keep the coven safe ... and everything in it."

"Did Gwendolyn have any sort of suspicions about Aunt Olivia?" I asked as I dusted off some dirt from the crumbling caves.

"I don't know. But I found the cave system to the High Coven sealed, so we will have to send a message if we want to speak to her."

"We'll sort this out, Jasper. I'll just have to find out who it is myself ... and quickly. The last thing I need is the Grand Coven on my case for something I know nothing about. But for now, let's get you home for some mackerel. You must be starving."

"I think we should look around while we're here," Jasper suggested. "The mackerel can wait. The bats may have dropped the potion somewhere near."

"You're right," I said, as we arrived at the cave's entrance. "Before we go, we should check the tributaries," I announced.

Amber turned to me. "For what?"

"A potion bottle," I replied.

Em stepped forward and shone her wand on my face. "What kind of potion are we talking about?"

"I'll explain when we get out of here."

38

"Well, you could at least tell us what it looks like," Scarlet said.

I looked to Jasper.

"It's a small silver flask," he said.

"A small silver flask," I relayed to the witches. "We will meet outside the entrance when you're done. And Jasper, you wait here and guard the entrance."

I set off through the cave, lighting every edge, only stopping for a moment to admire a stalactite formation that looked like a shimmering rainbow, turning almost every colour you could imagine as the light caught on the minerals found in the caves. I continued searching. But found nothing and headed back outside, where Jasper and the other witches stood waiting.

"No sign of it," I said.

"It's not your fault, Daisy." Jasper sauntered over to me. "I'll take the blame. But we should come back and look again. Crossover potions in the wrong hands ... that's more to worry about than what Gwendolyn will say."

A whoosh of air lifted my hair. "Gwendolyn ..." I said, under my breath.

"Merry Meet, witches," she greeted us. "It seems we have a problem." Her eyes flickered and widened before speaking again. "I want that potion, Daisy. And you're going to give it to me."

"We don't have it," I answered.

Gwendolyn scanned our group. "I'm glad you're not trying to deny it. I followed Jasper here but had to return to the High Coven." She extended her perfectly smooth hand out like a mother expecting a child to hand over a stolen sweet.

"I would," I began, "but a cauldron of bats stole it."

"A cauldron?"

"A cauldron," I repeated. "A group of bats ..."

"I know what a cauldron of bats is, Daisy." Gwendolyn retracted her hand and tapped her index fingers together as she looked at us suspiciously. "Well, the Grand Coven wants to speak to you, so find it. In the meantime, if I were you, I would stay out of the follies. Trouble like this is why the follies have guardians assigned to them. We have to know who is moving through them at all times."

"But we want to help," I said.

"I understand," Gwendolyn replied. "But without the proof that it is not you that is destroying the follies, the Grand Coven would never accept your help. They want someone held responsible. Find the potion, Daisy. And you had better come up with a plan ... quickly. Because time is only a luxury for witches" – her voice quietened as she pointed at each one of us on each word – "*who ... are ... not ... wanted ...* by the Grand Coven!"

Jasper lead us, single-filed, up the 77 steps towards the Folly Gate high street. The shop lights for Morton's Printers were off, but Morton had a habit of spontaneously appearing out of the alleyways. I kept my eyes peeled.

"Gwendolyn sounded pretty mad," Amber's voice came from behind me.

"She can be hard to read," I replied.

"But now we're all wanted by the Grand Coven?" Em asked.

I paused and looked back at them. "It seems like we are. But we'll have to find out what is going on ourselves, before we have to meet with the Grand Coven. I think the best idea is for us to stay together. That way, they can't accuse us of being somewhere we're not."

"Agreed," Scarlet said.

We continued up the stairs and along the high street when I noticed Winton, the chocolatier, working in his shop front window. His shop was not usually open so late, but I could never get enough of his lavender chocolate, and he kept a good supply. The aroma was always so inviting, making it impossible to pass without stopping in to buy his wares. I'm sure he did that on purpose.

"Let's stop here before we head home," I said.

"I hardly think it's the best use of our time," Em said. "How will chocolate help us?"

"I could give you a million reasons why chocolate helps in a tricky situation ..." I smirked.

Scarlet pulled the large oak door open. "He's more than just a simple chocolatier, Em," she said.

Winton greeted me with a smile as the buttery scent enveloped us. "Daisy ... welcome. I have your order right here." He beckoned us in as he walked across the shop and pulled a small paper bag from underneath the counter.

"You're working late today," I said as he passed the bag across the counter.

"Custom order," he said. "You know what that's like."

"I do. I have been receiving a lot of custom orders, but ... *Liv's Lumières* has been rather quiet."

"It's the same here, to be honest. After the murder at the Pentons', the footfall of tourists has been dropping. But I'm sure things will get back to normal soon ... I've put a free sample in there for you. A new recipe. Let me know what you think ... if I can get you away from the lavender chocolate."

"Thank you, Winton," I said as I passed him a jade coin.

"I knew it wouldn't take you long to decide what you wanted. My jade chocolate collection is rather eclectic ... something for everyone," he said. "Try not to eat it all at once."

"I'll do my best ... but you do make it difficult."

"I've worked very hard for that compliment." He chuckled as he looked across at my friends. "And Scarlet ... it's so good to see you. I haven't seen you around Folly Gate lately."

"Well, you are likely to be seeing more of me. I'm going to be staying with Daisy."

"Oh ... how lovely," his voice lifted in surprise. "Well, if you need anything, you know where I am."

"Thank you," she replied.

"Well, if there's nothing else ..." I said, "we'll leave you to get back to your orders." And I lifted my bag from the counter with a smile and a thank you, leaving the chocolate shop behind us, and continued on home ... with Jasper by my side.

CHAPTER SEVEN

A MBER STOOD IN FRONT of the bedroom door. "This room is perfect for me, Daisy."

"I'll find rooms for all of you," I said. "We've been renovating, but I—"

"It's perfect," she repeated as she turned the brass door handle and swung the door open. "See."

I stood for a moment before stepping into the room. "How did you ... It's beautiful, Amber ..."

"Thank you," she said, looking pleased with herself.

I walked across to the flower-filled windowsill and gently ran my finger along the underneath of a petal.

"Orange poppies," Amber said. "Not to be confused with the Californian poppy, of course. These are much better suited to our cooler climate." She picked up a small watering can and ceremoniously attended to the pots.

The orange poppy theme filled the room against a backdrop of clean, natural lines and furnishings. A rattan lampshade filtered a soft light across the room, and three tealight candles sat flickering on the small wooden bedside table. With a flick of her wand, she scattered the bed with cushions, and a cream-coloured wool blanket lay across its end.

I turned to Scarlet and Em standing in the doorway. "You can do this too?"

Scarlet nodded. "Most witches can. But from what I hear, you are still trying to do things the old-fashioned way. You have a wand for a reason, and you have a fine one at that. Maybe now you understand a little better. Your aunt didn't see a need to renovate this big old house. She would simply change it to suit her mood."

Em straightened her skirt. "You can't keep your feet in both worlds forever, Daisy. Eventually, you will have to choose."

Jasper stood at the end of the bed as if waiting for an invitation. Amber obliged by picking him up and setting him on the blanket. She looked down at Jasper and stroked the back of his neck. "I've never found my familiar. I've asked to be assigned ... but ..."

"You will," Scarlet reassured her. "They come and go as needed. Or in your case, Daisy ... they are passed on." Scarlet clapped her hands together. "Well, you look settled in here, Amber. Why don't you show us to our rooms, Daisy, and we can all get some rest?"

"Good idea," I said, as I took another look over the room. "I have to be up early to meet Ailsa, anyway. As unhappy as she's going to be when she hears about the Grand Coven, I think she might have something we may need."

My lessons in Ailsa's herbal room were a solemn affair. She took her work seriously, and I had begun to respect her *no-nonsense* approach. Looking back, it would be fair to say I had taken my first lessons with her for granted. Thinking I would be returning to London, I didn't give them the attention they deserved. But Ailsa persevered, and it wasn't long before I took the work more seriously too.

I arrived at her herbal room as she was setting up our lesson. Ailsa pushed her hands against the sturdy walnut table as she stood up and passed me a small jar filled with shiny black seeds. "I'm glad you have taken me up on my offer. Looking at the state of your seedlings … well, your herb garden will thank me for it. I'll show you how to use the seeds before you leave. But *today,* seeing as you have been completing your herbal potion lessons so quickly, I thought maybe it is time we moved into some new lessons."

"Really? Okay, I'm listening."

"Well, I think you're ready. Follow me. Jasper, you can come too. Your aunt always brought him with her."

Ailsa walked across the herbal room to a bare stone wall. I hadn't noticed before, but it was the only wall not filled with shelves of her drying herbs and paraphernalia. She pushed one stone back into the wall, then two … then three. And with an almighty push, she leant into the wall, revealing a room bubbling and steaming with coloured potions, shelved and labelled neatly in beakers and bottles. The potions ranged from bright reds and blues to hues of soft pinks and yellows, and my eye caught a hissing luminescent green liquid, coming from a row of open glass test tubes that hung from a small copper frame.

"Welcome to the Potion Room, Daisy." Ailsa held her hands up in a grand gesture. "And Jasper …" – she nodded – "welcome back."

"A potion room …" I said. We had only ever completed our lessons in her herbal room until now. "I've never seen anything like it."

Ailsa passed me a small bottle, filled with a dark green liquid. "You're progressing perfectly well with the Prime Spells, but potions are another matter. A witch with a dead greenhouse? Now, we can't have that! Take that potion I just gave you and put two drops at the base of each seedling, and they'll be back to themselves by morning. Do the same with the seeds I gave you and you'll have a kitchen garden ready before the end of the week.

As admirable as your endeavours are ... I hope you're not going to try to do things the hard way forever. What were you trying to grow in there, anyway?"

"Well ..." I recounted on my fingers. "Some *Poor Man's Treacle* ..."

"Good. I remember how difficult it was to convince you to read past 'Garlic' in your textbook."

"And Lupulus, Melissa, some Mary Gowles ... Elderflower ... oh, and Elf Leaf ..."

"Ah," she said. "You can never go wrong with Elf Leaf. Lavender is very useful in a witch's kitchen. And Elderflower, quite harmless, but if not prepared with care, it can have some serious side effects. Maybe we should cover that more in our next herbal lesson. It sounds like you're off to a good start. But before we look at the potions ... I know there's something on your mind."

I sat down in a high-backed wooden chair and tapped a glass vial filling up with liquid, dripping from a distillation setup. "I think you might be right about Morton. We are supposed to meet at his shop this morning. I've had some issues with the help he's been offering."

"Well, any witch will tell you that you can't rely on an alchemist." She wagged her finger in the air. "They're always sneaking about. How do you think he found you at the Folly Gate Fair? Sneaking – that's how."

"In his defence, I have to say he was helpful ... to an extent."

"They always are, but it's the price you pay for that help that brings the problems."

I took a deep breath. "I'm trying Ailsa. I really am. The Prime Spell Book brings a lot of responsibility. Sometimes I wonder if I should just give up and leave it unread. And go back to how things were – when I was free, free to travel, to catch up with friends ... to walk the city streets and complain about being bumped into. And sometimes I really miss not having to smile at anyone. No one smiles in London. They're all getting on with their business. In Folly Gate, it takes me half an hour to walk down the main street ... one smile and everyone wants to chitchat."

"Oh, don't be such a grump, Daisy. Everyone loves you here. The whole town has been supporting the shop, however they can. And as for missing the travel, Daisy, you've been abroad twice. I hardly think you're suffering from *wanderlust*."

"I like to keep my feet on the ground too, that's all. Not like some other people we know." I chuckled.

"I have to admit, Edlynn takes her floating about a bit too far sometimes." She smirked at me and walked over to put her hand on my shoulder. "You're going to do just fine in Folly Gate, Daisy. Give it some time and you'll see it is home. Let me see if I can find you a little potion ... maybe ..." She perused through her shelves of potions that swirled and changed colours like a celestial concoction after the birth of a star. "Yes. This might be a good one to introduce you to household potions."

She handed me a bulbous bottle filled with bright yellow liquid. As I turned it in my hand, swirls of silver stirred through the liquid until it became completely silver. "So pretty ..." I said as I sniffed the bottle.

"You won't smell anything ... or taste it, either. Just add one part potion to four parts of whatever you're drinking. You'll remember that, won't you Jasper?"

He meowed.

Ailsa continued, "But before we officially start our new potion lessons, I'll have to clear it with Gwendolyn. I'm sure there won't be a problem. The High Coven is always looking for new potion makers. And a witch can always use another scroll under her belt. The demand these days ... well, it keeps me busy, and I wouldn't say no to some help. In fact, I've got to take a potion to Gwendolyn. I don't know why she would need such a powerful potion, but a witch's business is her own ... especially when the one asking is the High Priestess. I'll ask her then. I fear we may lose many potion recipes if they're not being passed down. It used to be that the mentor would pass their recipes down to their apprentices, who would then pass them onto their apprentices ... all the way down the lines. But we are losing the potion maker lines. Witches want ready-made potions, nowadays. They want them ordered and delivered straight to their doors. They don't want to do the work ... I would be more than happy to start your new lessons whenever you're ready. We've covered most of the basics in your lessons so far, which will look good in Gwendolyn's eyes. Mastering potions is an art, and if placed in inexperienced hands ... well, sometimes it doesn't bear thinking about."

"Well ... It might be good for me to have something new to focus on ..." I said. "And seeing as it looks like my seedlings won't need as much work as first thought, I can make the extra time needed. What do you think, Jasper?" I asked him as I scratched the top of his head.

He looked up at me. "This is one scroll I wouldn't say no to," he said.

"Then it's a deal, Ailsa. You have a new apprentice."

"I'm happy to hear it." Ailsa smiled and passed me a new textbook. "Read the first three chapters before your next lesson."

I took the textbook, reading the title before placing it in my bag, "*The Hex-free Household.*"

"Yes. I thought it would be a good place to start. It looks like you are going to have more visitors, and it's best to be prepared."

"Well, I have three visitors at home now. Scarlet, Amber and Em are staying for a while. Until things settle down a little."

"Well, that book may be more useful than you think. Now, off you go. Enjoy that potion. It's one of my favourites. I'll let you know when we can move onto our next lessons."

"Thank you," I said as I collected my things. "But ... before I go ... there *was* one other thing I wanted to ask you."

"What is it?" she asked, as she replaced a potion on a shelf.

"I wondered if ... I mean, it's just an enquiry—"

"Well, spit it out," she said.

"I have a slight problem on my hands ... and I wondered if you could help me with ... a *crossover potion*?"

Ailsa looked at me in disbelief. "Well, Daisy. That sounds like more than a slight problem. But when it comes to potions of that manner ... the question is not *could* or *couldn't I* ... but *would* or *wouldn't I*?"

"I see. Then ... *would you*?" I asked.

Ailsa tilted her head and straightened her shoulders before answering, "I most definitely *would not*!"

Jasper meowed ...

CHAPTER EIGHT

I LEFT AILSA'S UNSURPRISED at her reaction. Maybe closing the divide between shadows and other witches would be harder than first expected. *And,* as my new house guests had proven they were more than capable of making themselves comfortable, Jasper took the short walk with me from Ailsa's house to *Liv's Lumières*. I opened the shop half an hour early and pottered, dusted and *wanded,* as I waited for Edlynn to arrive. A *wanding* of the shop sat right at the top of the *To-Do-List* when opening up. And Edlynn had been a patient teacher. A simple sweep with my wand got the shop tidy and neatened the shelves. The pottering and dusting – in her words '*all part of the illusion*'. Jasper found a comfy spot and curled up in the softness of the reading nook chair.

Edlynn arrived at 9am sharp, carrying her wicker basket over her arm. One side was overflowing with the familiar paper bags from *Home Sweet Scone*.

"Hungry this morning?" I asked.

"Their bakery has simply too much to choose from for breakfast." She proudly placed her basket on the counter with a cheeky grin. "I almost bought one of everything. They had baked some of their homemade crumpets this morning. I'll pop one in the toaster for you. And tea?"

"Just what I need." I smiled. "Thank you."

Edlynn had disappeared through to our small kitchen in the back of the shop as our first customer of the day arrived. She wheeled in a small floral suitcase behind her and set it to the side of the door before looking around. Her outfit had been chosen carefully with every detail complimenting her luggage, including a matching tote and sensible flat shoes for her journey.

I smiled. "Good morning. If there's anything I can help you with—"

"Yes," she said. "Maybe you can." Her voice was sweet but stern. "I'm looking for something for my daughter-in-law. I've come for a surprise visit for a few days."

"Oh, lovely," I said politely.

"Well, I'm sure my son will be happy to see me. Maybe you know him? Carol Watts."

I thought for a moment but no one came to mind. "I'm not sure I know a *Carol* ..."

"Oh, then maybe you know him as Detective Sergeant Watts."

"Sarge? Oh, yes, I know him. He agreed to let me work with his Detective Constable recently, on a case ... for research."

"Well, there you are. Folly Gate is such a small town. I would have thought most people would know him."

"Yes. Although, I wouldn't have pictured him as a *Carol* ..."

"It's a family name ... but he's never been particularly fond of it. I think he finds *Detective Sergeant* a much easier name to carry."

"I see. You know, I think I may have something you might like. It's new to our shop. I haven't even put it on the shelves yet. You could try it and let me know what you think? Let me get it from the back room."

I made my way past the counter to the back of the shop, and as I returned to the Sarge's mother, Edlynn emerged from the kitchen and placed two cups of tea on the counter. A curious look crossed her face as I handed the candle to our customer.

"Applewood and Rosemary," I said. "Place it on their mantelpiece, and when lit, it will fill the house with its cleansing fragrance."

She lifted it to her nose. "It smells delightful. She'll love it."

"I thought you might like it," I said, as I escorted her to the counter to wrap her gift. She took out her purse and looked across at Jasper, sleeping soundly on the chair.

"You wouldn't happen to be able to recommend something for removing cat hair, would you?" she asked.

Jasper lifted his head.

She leant in and whispered from behind her hand, "His wife is not the best of housekeepers, if you know what I mean. They have two British Shorthairs ... beautiful cats ... but notorious for their shedding."

I tried to hide my bemusement at her remark. *What a cheek.* "I'm sorry," I replied. "I don't have that problem. Our Jasper is low shedding."

Jasper blinked slowly at me, placed his head back down and closed his eyes.

"Oh. Well, lucky you," she said as I passed her the bag and closed the till.

"Yes ... *lucky* me," I replied.

"Well, thank you and I might see you around," she said as she extended the handle on her suitcase.

"Enjoy your stay." I lifted my hand to wave. If only she knew that the last thing you would ever want to call a witch is *lucky.*

Edlynn listened intently as I shared my recent conversation with Ailsa. I took the last bite of my orange marmalade topped crumpet, wiped my fingers on a napkin and took a sip of Earl Grey tea.

Edlynn stood up to take my empty plate. "Ailsa will come around, you'll see. And I'm sure when the time is right, more folly maps will turn up and you'll be able to figure out who is causing the damage."

"I hope you're right. I have to keep investigating the map I already have, I suppose. And I still haven't found out what that map was doing hidden in the Gamekeeper's Lodge on the Penton estate, either."

She reassured me, "Well, we three are a coven now ... and we'll help in any way we can."

"I still think about Morton's reaction to seeing the map at the fair ... and the *greed* in his eyes. He knew more than he was telling us."

"If you feel that strongly about it, why don't you talk to him? He is always around, *peddling* his wares ... especially to unsuspecting tourists. Speaking of tourists ... have you thought any further about what we might do for the Folly Gate Festival? Hopefully, the town will fill with tourists again, and we can put the nasty business of the Penton Estate murder behind us."

"I have some ideas," I said. "*Liv's Lumières* may be quiet ... the whole town is quiet. But now that I'm staying in Folly Gate, I intend to focus on the shop."

"Maybe you could have a new book out in time for the festival," Edlynn suggested. "Book signings can attract crowds ... especially for bestselling authors."

"I don't know. But maybe. I have a few spare drafts floating around. Anyway, as quiet as the town has been since the events at the Penton Estate, it *has* brought everyone together."

"I agree. Folly Gate has endured some hard times, but we always come through them." She placed our empty plates back on the counter. "And what about the Prime Spell Book? Any changes there? I can't help wondering what spells it is hiding. Maybe long-lost spells from centuries ago."

"Maybe. I haven't found anything new yet. But you and Ailsa will be the first to know. Interestingly, Jasper has been filling me in on my *line*. I never knew how awful it was in the past for witches. And imagining what the Banks witches before me went through … I won't take it for granted."

"Well, it's one reason Ailsa insists on studying the old arts … the *traditional* arts. A lot of witches these days are looking for *easy magic* instead of doing the work. *Ailsa* does the work."

"Yes, she told me … *more than once.*"

"Well, *I've* also been working on something new." Edlynn reached for her basket. "It's a little embarrassing because I'm not very good yet … but I've been learning to knit coats …"

"What's embarrassing about that? There's nothing better than snuggling into a warm knitted coat."

"*For cats …*"

I looked at Jasper. "*Coats*? Like for Jasper?"

"Yes," she said, rather coyly. "But I already tried to put one on him and he wouldn't let me near him." She pulled a small bedraggled-looking green knitted jumper from her basket. "I thought it was time to try knitting something more than a scarf."

"Oh, it's not so bad," I said. "Especially for a first try."

"I don't know. Maybe it's a non-starter. But I thought Kate might like them … for her wildlife hospital."

"I think that sounds like a great idea," I said, before turning to the reading nook. "Jasper? You didn't want to try on Edlynn's coat?"

He lifted his head. "No chance," he said. "I have my dignity to consider."

The tinkle of the shop bell interrupted our conversation.

"Imogen," Edlynn said. "Back so soon?"

"There's a problem with my order," she said, "and I'd rather discuss it somewhere a little more private – if you don't mind."

"I'm sorry. I'll sort it out for you straightaway," I said, as I gestured for her to follow me to the back room. "Come in and take a seat."

She handed me an opened package. "It's completely wrong, Daisy. It's not even close to what I ordered. I could have made it all the way back to Cornwall without even realising. I never had to second guess your aunt, but I'll be checking any order I get from you in the future."

I started flicking through my jade transaction book.

Imogen shifted in her chair. "I'm wondering if you might not have done it on purpose, Daisy. After all, you are supplying the Somerset covens. Someone could easily manipulate a young witch. I'd be careful with them, Daisy. You could destroy your aunt's legacy in an instant."

"And why shouldn't I supply the Somerset covens?" I asked.

"It doesn't surprise me they haven't told you," she scoffed.

"Told me what?"

"The reason this rift between the Cornish and Somerset Covens started."

"Well, a witch's business is her own ..."

"Well then, allow me to make it *your* business, too."

I looked up from my book. "Go ahead."

"Well ... it all comes down to Amethyst and Quartz. We have it, they want it, and we won't give it to them."

"*Amethyst and Quartz*? Surely they can get it from anywhere?"

"Yes, they can. But there is always demand for our highly sought-after gems and crystals, Daisy. Our amethyst is used extensively in wand making, and our quartz is some of the best in the world – very powerful. It enhances the power of any magical items – not to mention its healing properties.

And when the Somerset covens started ordering large amounts of quartz, we asked them what they were working on. After all, we are all a part of the Southern Covens. But they refused to respond. So, we refused to continue filling their orders. Their clientele has grown accustomed to a superior level of wands, but they can no longer craft them. And now, unfortunately, you are stuck right in the middle of it all. With us to the west of you and the Somerset covens to the north … there is only one way north for us, otherwise we have to detour through Dorset. And the Somerset witches make it as difficult as possible to pass through."

I took her opened package and placed it on the shelf for custom orders that were due to be collected. "I apologise again for the confusion, Imogen. Here, this is your order," I said, as I passed her the correct package. "And I hope you can come to some agreement soon with the Somerset witches."

"It would impress your aunt to hear you speak like that. She didn't choose sides either." Imogen took her time opening the package and checked over the items. "Everything seems to be here." She placed the package into her basket. "And Daisy … think about what I said. Alliances can strengthen you … just make sure you're on the right side. Merry Pass."

I smiled politely and opened the door. "You're welcome anytime and Merry Meet Again, Imogen." I held the door open for her to leave, but before I could close the door behind me, I heard her yell in a voice that could make the earth move.

"You!" Imogen took three long strides across the shop floor and stood chest to chest with Scarlet.

Edlynn looked at me and then back at the two women holding their stance. "Oh, this is not good timing," she said under her breath.

Imogen dropped her shopping basket to the floor.

I stepped over to the two women, their eyes not leaving each other's for a second. "Ladies," I said, "a witch's business is her own, remember? We would never disclose anyone's jade transactions ... not for any reason. As Edlynn said ... this is simply a matter of bad timing."

Edlynn spoke to the witches, "I don't want any kind of showdown in this shop. You will have to take that kind of business elsewhere ... otherwise, we won't be able to help you in the future. Do you understand?"

A voice came from the shop door. In the heat of the moment, none of us had heard the bell ring. "I hope I'm not interrupting anything ..."

"Jenifer," I said as calmly as I could manage. "No, not at all. What can we help you with?"

Imogen and Scarlet stood glaring at each other.

"Good," Jenifer said as she walked straight through the middle of the two witches, their eyes not leaving each other. "I wondered if you might put one of these posters in your shop front window. My event company is going to host murder mystery nights at the Folly View Hotel."

Edlynn took the poster from her and looked it over. "Do you think it is such a good idea? The town has been so quiet since the murder case on your estate—"

"All publicity is good publicity," Jenifer said. "Isn't that what they say?"

Imogen broke her stance and walked over to Jenifer. "That's a beautiful necklace you are wearing. I've never seen that shade of topaz before. Although, I have seen something similar ... but not nearly as bright. Where did you find a necklace like that?"

Jenifer looked taken aback and clasped the pendant in her hand. "Thank you. It was a gift ... from my grandmother ... given to me a long time ago now ... I've had it since I was a child."

"Ah, a priceless treasure then," Imogen said.

"Yes." Jenifer shifted her posture uncomfortably before turning her attention back to us. "So, the poster?"

"No problem," I replied.

"Good. We'll have Folly Gate back on its feet in no time." She took a quick glance at Imogen and Scarlet and made a beeline for the door.

Imogen picked up her basket. "Remember what I said, Daisy." She looked Scarlet dead in the eye and turned to us before leaving. "Merry Pass, ladies."

Edlynn replied in unison with me, "Merry Meet Again."

Scarlet waited for Imogen to leave before speaking, "I would be careful believing everything I hear, Daisy. That cauldron is going to boil for a long time, and I don't see it cooling off anytime soon."

I paused before breaking the silence, "I understand. So, onto other matters, how did you sleep? I left before you woke this morning."

"Very comfortably, thank you. I thought I'd stop in and let you know we would all be out of the house today. I'm going to speak to some friends and look for any clues of use to us. And Amber and Em are heading off to a *Gathering* tonight. They thought it might be a good place to start, and see if there are any rumours floating around about the follies."

"Good, that should be helpful," I said.

Edlynn clasped her hands together. "Well, I *snap imaged* Imogen and couldn't find anything."

"You don't feel strange doing that to someone?" I asked her. "Intruding on someone's thoughts?"

"A *snap image* spell doesn't intrude on thoughts ... it only passes me a quick image ... like a photograph. It's all I need. And it has to be precisely at the time they have the image in their head. Sometimes it's a totally useless spell ... capturing only boring little daydreams or the like. But under the right circumstances and with good timing, it can be very helpful indeed. I think you're a few scrolls away from that spell, though."

Scarlet smirked a little dangerously. "Well, it won't take Daisy long, I'm sure." She reached into her pocket. "I wanted to see if you have some supplies for a full moon ritual. Nothing too extraordinary. A couple of potions, and some incense, oils, brews ...”

“That shouldn’t be a problem,” Edlynn said.

Scarlet passed her a list. “Well, I better get a move on,” she said to me. “But I’ll meet you at home tonight? Amber and Em will be out late, I expect.”

“I’ll see you then,” I replied.

“How exciting for them,” Edlynn said. “I’ve always loved a good *Gathering*. You just never know who you might run into.”

Chapter Nine

E DLYNN SAT ON THE stool behind the counter, casting on stitches for another attempt at a knitted coat. I placed the last piece of tape on the corner of Jenifer's poster and ran my finger along the small typeface across the bottom.

PRINTED BY MORTON'S PRINTERS

"I'd be careful about that sort of alliance, Daisy," Edlynn said. "Alchemists hold their secrets – like we do. But there is always a price to pay to them. There were times when the craft was being diligently extinguished, and they were only concerned with what they could gather for the Order."

"But if Aunt Olivia was working with him, there must be a reason, right? He might be of some help."

"Well, your aunt knew how to hold her own ... but then ... so do you, Daisy."

I walked over and positioned the poster on the front window. "I think she'll be happy with it there – *front and centre*. Just as she likes it." I laughed.

Edlynn grinned.

I made my way back to the counter and stacked a small pile of envelopes. "I'm going to run these down to the Post Office. And I want to stop in and see Penelope Black. I'm hoping we can get a stall for the Folly Gate Festival. I thought it would be a good way to bring people up to the shop."

"I like it. Penelope is worth having on your side. Not a lot of business happens in Folly Gate without her approval, when it comes to the Parish Council. Especially if you ever need planning permission or the likes ..." Edlynn paused her knitting. "It will get easier, Daisy. I know it can be difficult moving somewhere different from where you're used to, but you have to get out there, instead of spending your time torturing yourself by renovating that house. It will take you years at the rate you're going. We really don't understand why you don't use your wand more."

"I know, Edlynn. Actually, my houseguests have been showing me what a little *wanding* at home can do."

Edlynn's face dropped. "Oh. That's nice."

I caught her look. "And I would love for you and Ailsa to help me, if you have the time, of course."

Her face lifted. "We have all the time in the world for you, Daisy." She smiled and went back to counting her stitches.

I was about to leave when a petite woman entered the shop, adjusting her *boho-chic* tote and looking around as the door closed behind her. She pushed her glasses back up onto the bridge of her nose and walked across the shop floor towards us.

"Daisy Banks?" she asked.

"Yes," I replied. "Is there something I can help you with?"

She adjusted her scarf nervously. "I heard you had moved to Folly Gate, and I didn't quite believe it, but after some research, I found it was true."

"Oh, well, you found me." I smiled. "How can I help?"

She started rummaging through her tote, emptying some of its contents on the counter before pulling something out wrapped in a red and blue silk scarf. "I hope you don't mind …" She placed the item on the shop counter and unwrapped it. "It's a first edition," she said.

My shoulders softened. "*Criss Cross Croissant*. One of my better books," I said.

"Oh, it's my favourite. I was hoping to get it signed at your book signing in London, but the line was so long, and you had to leave … so I never got it signed. I wondered … seeing as I was in town … if you might?"

Her voice was soft, almost timid. There was no way I would say no. "Of course. Who should I make it out to?"

"Oh, thank you. Make it to Amie – with an *i* … *e*."

I signed the book and passed it back to her.

Edlynn sensed her awkwardness. "Are you in town for long, Amie?"

"Oh, a few more days. It's a friend's birthday on the weekend. I thought I'd come down earlier and take in the sights."

"Well, Folly Gate is happy to have you visit," Edlynn said.

"Thank you." She pointed at her vintage *Leica* camera hanging around her neck. "There are some beautiful landscapes here. I'm hoping to catch a *golden hour* or two if I can."

"You're a photographer?" I asked.

"No. It's a hobby for now. I'd never be brave enough to publish."

"We all have to make our first submission at some point," I said. "And although it's a little terrifying at first, it's worth it in the end. If you take any exciting photos while you're here, let me know. I have a friend at the Folly Gate Gazette."

"Thank you," she said with a smile. "Maybe I will."

"When is your friend's party?" Edlynn asked.

"Saturday night," Amie replied. "My friend used to be a kind of *festival and cider girl* … but now she's married to her wildlife hospital."

"Do you mean Kate?" I asked her.

"Yes, you know Kate?"

"Folly Gate is a small town," I said. "Yes, we know her, and we'll be there on Saturday, too."

She smiled. "Well, then it seems I've come to the right place to look for a gift for her."

"I'm sure we have something Kate would love," I said. "But I am just on my way out, so I will leave you in Edlynn's hands ... and I'll see you, Amie, on Saturday night."

Edlynn ushered her over to our gift hampers filled with assorted soaps, candles, lotions, bath bombs and oils. Jasper arched his back and stretched *big* before casually slinking off the sofa and following me out of the shop.

We made our way across the High Street and down the 77 steps towards Morton's shop. Jasper stayed close behind me. "We're going to pay Morton a visit first," I said.

"Well, I will follow you wherever you go," he said. "Your aunt liked to use his services, but she was very wary of him and the Order. And your grandmothers have had little success seeking their advice. His predecessors don't carry the best of reputations."

"Well, the shop is open. I know there have to be more maps and I am sure he knows about them. They have passed that shop down through his family for over two hundred years."

"I think it's been around longer than you think. It hasn't always been called Morton's Printers. He changed that himself. And it wouldn't surprise me if you found an old copy of *The Canterbury Tales* stashed around there somewhere."

I opened the heavy door to his print shop. His ostentatious suede hat, decorated with a green sash and red feather, hung on a brass hook alongside his long-waxed coat.

"Good morning, Morton," I said.

"Daisy. Come in. I thought you might visit soon. I've been hearing good things about you."

"Oh, that's always nice, I suppose," I replied.

"Yes, yes, it is. I've been hearing rumours it was you that found the Penton Estate murderer."

"Well, that's hardly a rumour, Morton. It made the headlines in the Folly Gate Gazette."

"That's not what I'm talking about, Daisy. I'm talking about rumours that move more in *our circles* ... rumours about how you found him. Folly Gate Fair may not be open all the time, but there are people who can get in there as easily as you can. I think you should be more careful in the future. You never know who's watching you."

He looked me straight in the eye, and I had to wonder if it wasn't him who had been doing the sneaking around *or* the person who started the rumours.

"What rumours are you talking about?" I asked him.

"Well, I may as well tell you. I suppose you will find out soon enough, anyway. Rumours, by nature, usually always find their way back around to the *rumee*."

"That's not even a word, but I'm getting used to being the talk of the town. My aunt had quite the reputation, and it seems to follow me more than the rumours do."

"These rumours are more specific – about the follies ..."

"What do you mean *follies*? You know I have a map of the follies and can use them whenever I please."

"Ah, well." He wagged his finger in the air. "You have *a* map ... of *a* folly. And may I remind you that you could only see it using my tools?"

"Do you see what I'm talking about now?" Jasper asked. "He doesn't know you have folly sight. He thinks you still need his tools to see the map.

I would keep that to yourself for now. Alchemists ... they never help for the sake of helping. They wait patiently and quietly until you come looking for them. They know you want something from them ... and it never comes cheap."

Morton looked down at Jasper. "Rather chatty today, aren't we?" He looked back at me. "I suppose he is warning you about the repercussions of working with alchemists ... in the past. But I can see that although your aunt's reputation follows you, you are not her. You are your own person. We are similar in that way. My family's reputation follows me too. But I also have different dreams and desires for my work. I am not my father. However, I have a lot of paraphernalia he has passed down to me. And like you, I will do whatever it takes to protect it. I know alchemists and witches have always been at odds with each other, but if we were to forge a good working relationship, who knows what we might discover?"

"I suppose I could consider it," I said. "What do you have in mind?"

"Follow me," he said as he eagerly removed a large keyring from underneath his desk. We followed him to an ordinary door at the back of his shop. He placed his key into the old, warded lock and turned it hard. "Now, watch your step."

The air became colder with every step of the worn-down stone stairway. Jasper walked ahead of me. I heard the strike of a match and caught Morton's bearded silhouette as he lit a large pewter and glass lantern. "My laboratory," he said as he nodded proudly.

I stepped closer to the heavy table in the middle of the room. Shelves extended out on every wall, filled with boxes and bottles labelled with words like *ligna, sulphura, varia* and *mineralia*. Above the shelves hung tortoise shells and swordfish teeth, and statues of bears and skulls and couples embracing.

Jasper sauntered around the room before coming back to my side.

"I want to show you something, Daisy," Morton said. "Something you might help me with. And then, to make our agreement fair, we could discuss something I might help you with."

"Agreed," I said.

He cleared a space on his table before opening a cedar cabinet and sliding out a drawer. "I want you to look at this."

He turned to place the large print on the table, but before he even had time to place the glass paperweights on the edges, I gasped.

"I knew you had the sight!" he exclaimed. "I knew it! What do you see?"

I leant over the table and traced my fingers across the parchment. "I'm sorry, Morton. I don't see anything."

"Ah, I understand," he said. "We agreed to a fair deal, so a fair deal it is. Is there something I might help you with?"

"There may be," I said as I stepped back from the table. "What do you know about *crossover potions*?"

"Ah, very rare ... and a dangerous thing indeed. That's what I know."

"We lost one. And I need another."

"You had one? Where did you get it?"

"I would never say," I replied.

"I understand. Well, if you can help me with the map, I may be able to help you find a potion."

He turned and fumbled with some boxes on his shelves. "You'll need one of these," he said, as he passed me a small pebble with a hole in it. "*And this ...*" He unlocked a cabinet and passed me a small bottle. "*Raphael's pigment*," he said. "You take those items and when you get what you need, come back to me and I'll give you the map. You'll see that you can trust me ... and we can share what we find ... *together*."

"And what am I supposed to do with these items?"

"I'll explain it all to you: for potions as dangerous as you're looking for, you need to meet with someone just as dangerous. Do we have a deal?"

I reached out my hand.

Jasper moved in. "Shaking hands with an alchemist is a binding agreement, Daisy. And I've never heard of a way to break it."

"We have a deal," I said. "Don't make me regret it. Now, where do I go for a crossover potion?"

"For a deal like that, you need …" – he paused – "the Artist."

"The Artist?"

"Yes. The one who lives in the small house. The one who painted your aunt."

CHAPTER TEN

I SPENT THE REST of the day contemplating Morton's offer. And after a quick dinner and mackerel for Jasper, I spent some time in what was quickly becoming my favourite room in the house. I placed my head against the soft bath pillow and stayed there until my fingers wrinkled. After stepping out of the hot bath, I wrapped myself in a warmed robe. My bathroom was an oasis of jasmine steam, and I curled my toes into the plush bathmat as a quiet instrumental played on hidden speakers. Baskets filled with trailing plants hung from every corner, and the soft candlelight reflected in the mirror. The weight of the day lifted from my shoulders ... for a moment.

"Best get back to it," I said aloud. I picked up my wand sitting on my antique ceramic shelf, and with a simple swirl in the air, the bath water drained, the steam cleared, and the music softened. "Maybe Edlynn and Ailsa are right, after all."

I opened the door to find Jasper on the landing and Scarlet taking the last stairs up to the floor.

"Oh, there you are," she said. "I just got in. Ooh, I love what you've done with the bathroom."

"Thank you." I smiled. "I was thinking of changing into my pyjamas and treating myself to a strawberry and cream prosecco, if you're interested."

"I'll meet you downstairs," she replied with a glint in her eye.

I walked to my bedroom and pulled out my favourite flannelette PJs, breathing in their lavender scent and looking out of the large bay window and across the moors. As I had rekindled the fire and sprinkled nettles on it before bathing, I left my feet bare.

I made my way down to the kitchen, passing Jasper taking in the fire's warmth. As I pulled out two cocktail glasses, Scarlet entered wearing a pair of silk white pyjamas covered in deep red roses. Her hair was pulled up in a messy bun, and she had covered her face in a bright green mud mask.

"It sounded like a *girl's night in* to me," she said.

"I suppose it is," I said with a smile. "Ailsa gave me a pillow dream potion. Would you like some ... with your cocktail?"

"Yes, why not? I haven't had one of them in the longest time."

I popped the cork of a bottle of Cara's prosecco.

"It's almost like we have something to celebrate," Scarlet said.

"Maybe we do," I said as I added chopped strawberries to our glasses. "I went to see a friend today who might help us find out who has been using crossover potions. And he gave me a fae stone and some rare pigment. He told me I'm to take it to the man in the small house. He's an artist, apparently."

"I can't say I know much about that. But I know that messing with fae can cost a lot of jade. We try to only use fae if we need them. Their games are rarely worth the hassle. But if I can be of any help, let me know."

"Thanks," I said as I passed her the cocktail.

She raised her glass. "Here's to new friends ... and old allies."

I clinked her glass and took a sip.

"Ooh, this is good." Scarlet giggled and took another sip. "*Really good* ..." She giggled again.

"It is," I said. "The strawberries ... the ice cream ..."

"What about them?" she asked, stifling another giggle.

"Well, you see here. You've got the strawberries …" I took another sip.

"And the ice cream …" She snorted.

"Yes, that's what I said … the strawberries …" But I could no longer hold it in. My shoulders loosened and my foot started tapping.

"Here we go. A good old-fashioned pillow dream potion!" Scarlet squealed as she spun her way into the sitting room. "We need some music!"

I snapped my wand at my aunt's old stereo, and the electro swing sounds of *Caravan Palace* filled the room. A sight that would impress Edlynn.

We danced and sipped in front of the warm fire. Our feet would not stop. Scarlet jumped on the sofa and bounced about, kicking her legs as high as she could, almost losing balance, and collapsing in laughter. Even Jasper joined us, racing in circles, jumping over the table and dancing around on his two back paws.

A loud knock on the front door stopped me mid high kick. I pointed my wand at the stereo to stop the music and froze with Scarlet, as if we were in the middle of a game of musical statues. The only sound was the squeaking of the chandelier as Jasper swung back and forth, held on only by his small extended claws.

"Who's that, Jasper?" I asked him as he held on to listen, before letting go and landing on his feet … *of course.*

"Ethan …" Jasper said.

"What's he doing here? I haven't seen him for weeks."

"That's probably the reason he's here, Daisy," Jasper said. "You *have* been keeping to yourself lately."

"Right, well, I better get the door then."

"Yes … you better," he said.

Scarlet let out a little 'woo' before adjusting her pyjamas and plonking herself on the sofa.

"I won't be a minute," I said, as I walked to the front door. I took a breath to compose myself before opening it. "Ethan ..."

"That's quite a smile, Daisy," he said. "I haven't caught you in the middle of something, have I?"

"Me? Umm ... no. Not at all. Come in." The pillow dream potion must have been written all over my face.

"Okay ..." He looked around the corner like he was expecting someone to be there.

"It's just me, my friend, Scarlet ... and Jasper, of course."

Ethan looked at the open bottle of prosecco. "Oh, I'm sorry ... I *have* caught you in the middle of something."

"No, no, no. We've only had one glass. My friend from London sent me a few cases of prosecco. Apparently, her family's chain of hotels is going to be stocking it ... *exclusively*. She asked for my opinion and to pass it around. Here, I'll get you a bottle." I tried to stifle a giggle.

Ethan smirked. "Well, it certainly looks to me like you may have had more than one."

"Well ... always the detective, aren't you, Ethan?" I teased. "There's plenty there for you to join us for one if you like. Or were you here on a more serious matter?" I leant on the kitchen bench for some balance, but my elbow slipped under the weight.

"I have to say, I don't think I've ever seen you like this."

"I thought it was time to let my hair down a little – you know, lighten up."

"Well, it's good to see you happy. The reason I dropped by was because I haven't seen you around. I just wanted to see how you were."

"I appreciate it. But as you can see, all is well. Not a lot to tell, really. Although, I have a party this weekend. Maybe you're going? It's for Kate ... who runs the wildlife hospital."

"Unfortunately, I'm on duty this weekend."

"Oh, that's a shame. She's hired a paddle steamer on the River Dart."

"It sounds like a lot of fun." He patted his back pockets. "Well, I'll let you get back to your friend. I'm glad to see everything is okay."

"Oh, my friend. Yes. Well, at least let me introduce you before you go."

"Sure," he said as he followed me through to the sitting room.

After a quick, polite introduction, we followed Ethan back to the front door.

"Are you sure you won't stay?" I asked him.

"Thanks," he said. "But I know a *girl's night in* when I see one." He smiled. "We'll catch up soon. Enjoy your night."

I gently closed the door behind him and turned to Scarlet.

"He seems nice," she said with a cheeky grin.

"Oh, it's nothing like that." I waved off her look. "We were childhood friends, but we lost touch when I left Folly Gate. We recently worked on the Penton case together."

"Oh, I see." Scarlet looked curious. "Some friendships are like that. You just pick up where you left off."

"Yes, I suppose it's like that."

"So … why did you leave Folly Gate? I mean, it seems like home to you and not everyone has that."

"I had no choice. After my mother died, my aunt Olivia offered to help look after me while my father got on his feet. We stayed here for a few years, but then he took a job in London and we moved. When you're a child, you don't really ask questions. We never came back here, and he never said why. But from what I am finding out about our family, I think he was simply trying to protect me … from all of this."

"Well, you don't have to face this on your own, Daisy. You have us now."

"I know. And I'm grateful."

Scarlet placed a reassuring arm around my shoulders and gave them a slight squeeze. "Let's talk more about this another time. We should get some sleep."

I agreed and made my way upstairs. Jasper curled up on the corner of the bed and purred. "Goodnight, Jasper," I said, as I laid my head down on the pillow and pulled my duvet up tight. And before I could say another word, I closed my eyes ... and dreamed until morning.

CHAPTER ELEVEN

W E AGREED TO MEET at Edlynn's to get ready for Kate's party. I took the short walk, with Jasper at my heels, and found myself surprised at how easily I could recognise the distinct chirping of robins, as they darted back and forth through the hedges and shrubs of Folly Gate. When I arrived at Edlynn's cottage, she had laid out a board of savoury snacks on her delicately decorated front room table. Nothing too filling: some cashews, pistachios and almonds, with freshly quartered bright red Royal Gala apples, water crackers and a local Sharpham cheese.

She passed me a flute of prosecco. "It will loosen the spirits," she said.

"From what Daisy told us earlier, it sounds like she had enough of that last night," Ailsa said.

"We only had one glass ..." I said, as I raised my drink. "By the power of three."

"The power of three," they repeated back to me.

"You may have had only one glass, Daisy," Ailsa said. "But mixed with that potion ... well, now you know. I *had* thought you might enjoy it with a nice chamomile tea or similar before bed."

Edlynn smacked her lips together. "You'll have to tell Cara I approve of her prosecco. I can taste notes of lemon ... maybe a little pear ..." She took another sip.

"And what do you know about prosecco?" Ailsa asked.

"Not much at all," she said. "Except that apparently the bubbles don't last as long as champagne ... But, onto the important matters: what are we going to wear to Kate's party? Definitely something like the *flapper girls* would wear, I think. Come over to my mirror, Daisy."

Edlynn stood me in front of her mirror, straightened my shoulders and flicked out her wand. "How about this?"

A swirl of air rushed over my body, and the mirror filled with bright floating colours, twisting and turning like a thousand tornadoes.

"Nearly there," she said. "*And* ... what do you think?"

The colours faded from the mirror, and I stood dressed in a black fringed mid-calf dress. It had gold and emerald-green peacock feathers beaded into its black tulle overlay, with an olive-green lining which sparkled under the light. I pivoted on my toes, inspecting the black stockings and buckled low-heeled shoes. "But Edlynn ... my hair! What have you done?"

"Oh, Daisy ..." Edlynn shook her head. "Don't panic. It is only temporary. What do you think? Look, even your stocking line is straight."

I ran my hands down the dress and stroked my short, black bobbed hair. "Well, it does kind of suit me, don't you think?"

Edlynn grinned. "Absolutely. You look fabulous, Daisy! My magic wouldn't have it any other way."

Ailsa nodded in approval. "Very nice."

"Then it's settled," Edlynn said. "Flapper girls it is!"

Ailsa took her turn in front of the mirror, stepping away in an elegant silver and black dress, complete with long pewter gloves and a rhinestone headpiece.

Edlynn clapped her hands in delight at her work before taking her turn in front of the mirror. "Ready ..." she said, "and Ta dah!"

She stood before us in long tan trousers with blue and red braces over a crisp white shirt. A flat cap sat neatly on her perfectly curled blonde hair, with tri-coloured brogues on her feet and a replica *tommy gun* poised in her hands. "What do you think?" She laughed. "The gangster look!"

"For Thomas, maybe," I said, with a chuckle. "Speaking of Thomas, did you ask him to come tonight?"

Edlynn spun back around to the mirror. "He couldn't make it. He has to work … a conference, I think."

And before I could ask any more questions, she had turned back around to us, dressed in a beautiful red dress with layers of diagonal fringe and a matching feathered headband. "Here, Daisy, I forgot to give you this." She tossed me a long black boa. "Let's get going. We don't want to miss the train. Kate said it was leaving at 5:17pm."

"Thanks," I said as I wrapped the feather boa around my neck. "But before we go, I wanted to talk to you about something."

Edlynn began filling her small clutch purse for the evening. "What is it?"

"I went to see Morton," I said.

"Disappointing," Ailsa said. "But, nonetheless, what did he have to say?"

"He has a map …" I said.

"What kind of map?" Edlynn asked as she checked her lipstick in the mirror.

"A folly map. I only saw it for a moment. But it is much larger than the one I found at the Penton's. This one not only mapped follies from county to county but, in the quick look I had, it seemed to map follies from country to country too. He said I could have it if I take something to the man in the small house."

"Well, that map *would* help," Edlynn said.

Ailsa picked up her bag. "One meeting with an alchemist, and you're already running errands for him."

I looked at Edlynn. "Will you help me?"

"Of course," she said without hesitation. "Are you any closer to finding out who is in the follies? Who do you think it could be? I know most witches in the Southern Covens. And I couldn't imagine any of them wanting to destroy the follies. Especially when we have a witch in our coven that can move through them so freely. You would think everyone would realise it gives us an advantage over other covens ... Imagine what else we might find as you open more of them."

"It's quite a mystery," Ailsa said. "I too would have thought everyone would want to be working together to make the most of them ... I mean, in theory, you could travel across the country in little more than a twinkle in your eye."

"I don't know any more about the follies, yet," I said. "And maybe it's fair that Gwendolyn is holding me up to scrutiny. I *am* the new witch in town, after all. And I suppose I haven't been all that enthusiastic about the *craft* in the past. But I'm determined to show her I am loyal to the covens. And, if you want to hear it, I think I could have an idea about how I might convince her."

Chapter Twelve

I HELD ONTO THE chain railing as I walked up the gangway to be greeted by the captain. He stood with his pristine white hat, smiling and nodding politely as he welcomed everyone onto the paddle steamer. Edlynn walked in front of me, carrying a small, wrapped gift for Kate, and Ailsa had offered to carry the basket of thoughtfully arranged prosecco – at least I could tell Cara I was getting the word out. And *I* carried a dried flower cloche with weaved gold ribbon around its base.

"I'll get someone to take those gifts for you," the captain said as we approached.

With a simple glance to his side, a steward came and relieved Ailsa of the weight of her basket, and she directed us across to a gift table.

"You made it!" Kate's voice sung across the paddle steamer's dining room. "Thank you so much for the gifts. You really didn't have to ... Let me show you where to get a drink. I created a signature cocktail for tonight and called it a *Gangster Rose*. Prosecco with a little damson syrup for some zing, and the rose ... well, you'll love it, I'm sure."

Edlynn walked to Kate's side as we made our way to the bar. "I'm so used to seeing you wearing your wellington boots and jeans, Kate. It's a pleasant surprise to see you in such a beautiful dress."

"Oh, thank you, Edlynn," she said. "It's true, I don't get to dress up as much as I would like anymore, but I never turn down a chance. And thank you for getting into the spirit of things. You all look gorgeous! Well, I shall leave you in Andrew's expert hands. He makes the best cocktails, and when you're ready, feel free to explore the paddle steamer. She's beautiful." She waved at a friend arriving and disappeared off to mingle with her guests.

"She seems right at home," Ailsa said. "I always thought of Kate as more of a down-to-earth person, but she does seem to come alive at a party."

"Like you at a fair." I smirked.

Ailsa scanned the room. "I'm not really one for parties."

"We know," Edlynn said.

As Andrew shook up our cocktails and poured over the prosecco, I looked around at the grand room. Every table had black and silver helium-filled balloons for centrepieces and rose vines spiralling up glass vases. Kate had picked the perfect venue for her theme. Every detail shone in brass and black and gold. They set the tables with ice buckets filled with unopened bottles of prosecco, waiting for the celebration to begin.

The paddle steamer's powerful whistle blew. "We must be setting off," Edlynn said. "Let's head out on the deck."

We walked together as we passed the words *Queen of the Dart*, meticulously carved and stained into the teak on the boat's name plaque. The shining brass rails and polished wooden deck gleamed under the setting sun. I could hear the pistons firing up and whooshing and whirring as the large red paddle slowly turned. It continued to stop and start until it gained full momentum and carried us away from the riverbank. The spirits of the party guests lifted, their smiling faces and laughing blending with the soft jazz music – everyone but our Ailsa. I'm sure she would have much rather been at home pottering in her herbal room. And as for Jasper, *no cat policies* on paddle steamers meant he missed out on being the life of the party. But then cats and water … they're not always a welcome mix.

We mingled and made polite conversation as they passed around canapes, from goat's cheese and fig tartlets to *prosciutto crudo* wrapped pears and wild mushroom cups. An oyster bar set up on deck with a serving table filled with rock salt offered you a choice of shucked natural oysters with fresh lemon, or Rockefeller's and Kilpatrick's, baked fresh in the galley.

"This must have cost a fortune," Ailsa said to us.

"Well, you only turn thirty once," Edlynn replied. "Why don't you just enjoy it, Ailsa? Let the breeze blow through your hair ... and the scent of the river fill your nostrils—"

"Oh, you do go on, Edlynn," Ailsa said as she sipped her cocktail.

"Well, I'm off to have a good time then," Edlynn said.

Ailsa huffed as she took a seat on a long wooden bench and looked out across the river.

"You didn't have to come," I said, as I joined her.

"I know," Ailsa answered. "But sometimes we have to make an effort. These sorts of *soirees* have never really interested me. I don't understand the point. There's no effort on the host's part. It's just paying to entertain your guests. It's all for show. There's no love in it."

"Not like our parties at home?"

"Yes, I suppose."

"Aha! So, you *do* love us," I teased. "I knew it!"

She dabbed the condensation on her cocktail glass with a napkin. "You've become ... *tolerable* ... I suppose ..." – she winked – "now, why don't you go and catch up with Edlynn? Enjoy yourself. I'm going to sit here for a moment."

"Do you want me to get you anything?"

She waved me off with her hand. "No, no. Thank you. I don't want to spoil the dinner."

I turned and took in a long breath. The damp smell of the riverbanks filled the air, and I was walking to the edge of the deck to take it in when a voice came from behind me, "I thought it was you. I came in yesterday ... to get a present for Kate."

"Amie," I said. "It's nice to see you again."

"You have a good memory. I'm terrible with names," she said as she pulled a small glass dropper bottle from her bag and squeezed three drops of liquid under her tongue. "I don't really have sea legs," – she lifted the bottle – "this seems to help. Flower essences – I make them myself. They work by using the energetic vibrations of the flower."

I smiled politely. "It sounds very interesting," I said. "Well, isn't it a lovely party?"

"I told Kate it would be fun. But it took some convincing."

"How so?" I asked.

"Kate wanted a simple spit roast buffet for her birthday. There is a pub—"

"She's probably talking about The Cidered Apple. John has a reputation for his food. Good old-fashioned pub grub."

"But I said to her that she had been sitting on her money long enough. It's time to enjoy it a little. She spends all her money and time in that wildlife hospital. I'm glad I convinced her to have this party. I even got her to agree to let me choose the menu. Otherwise, you would probably be eating roast beef and Yorkshire puddings tonight."

"Well, I have to say I would have no complaints about that, anyway. And Kate looks like she's having a good time."

"She is. You know what they say ... 'party like it's your last' ... or was that 'live each day like it is your last' ... or something about dancing in a storm ... Oh, I don't know." She laughed. "It looks like someone's trying to get your attention."

I turned in the direction she was pointing. "Oh, that's my friend, Dawn. I didn't know she would be here. Shall I introduce you?"

"Sure, why not?"

Dawn looked impeccably dressed, as expected for these kinds of events. But it has to be said, she wasn't afraid of getting her hands dirty either. Her stables weren't the only thing that needed *mucking out* on the Penton Estate.

"I love your dress," Amie said to Dawn.

"Thank you," she replied politely. "It took some work to get into."

"I can imagine. Is it vintage? The bodice work is stunning."

"It was my great grandmother's. It's been tucked away, but I've had my eyes on it for years. I thought it would be perfect for this occasion. I love to imagine what she got up to in this dress ... where she went, who she spoke with. From the looks of your rings and pendant ... *and* that scarf, you look like you know your way around a vintage shop yourself."

"It's one of my favourite things to do. You never know when you'll find a treasure." She lifted her camera. "Shall I take a photo of you two together? I'll get a copy to you."

"Sure," we said together and leant in for the shot.

Amie's camera made a single flash burst. "Well, I'll let you two catch up," she said. "I need to speak with Kate before dinner is served. It was nice to meet you, Dawn."

The thunderous roar of the steam paddle drowned out any quiet conversation, but Edlynn's laugh could be heard over everything. Thomas would have loved dancing the night away with her.

"I think I might have had my fill of damson and rose prosecco," Dawn said as she looked around. "I don't see any signs for the *Ladies*."

"Come on," I said. "We'll find them together."

We walked along a short wooden corridor, with our drinks in our hands. Dawn popped her head around an open door. "That must be the bridge ... or do they call it the helm on these?" she said.

"Dawn, someone's coming."

We stepped back to let the woman carrying a tray of empty glasses through. "Can I help you?" she asked abruptly.

"We were looking for the *Ladies*," Dawn asked politely.

The woman plastered a smile on her face. "Back out here, take a left and you'll see them in front of you."

"Thank you," I said, as she left. "Oh, Dawn. Is that one of your buttons?" I bent down and picked up a silk fabric covered button.

"It might be," she said as she checked over her dress. "But I can't see from where ..."

A man's deep voice came from behind the open door, "Why don't you two get on with your job? And I'll get on with mine."

A woman's voice replied, "If you keep this up, Albert, we are going to lose everything. There was a time when we were the most important things to you, but it doesn't look like we are anymore."

"Oh, leave it," he said. "I've had enough of being nagged by you two. Leave me alone and let me get on with my job."

We heard footsteps heading towards us. I pretended to fumble and find where Dawn's button was missing from on her dress. The woman stopped for a moment and looked us up and down. I held the button up feebly. "Lost button ..." I said.

Chapter Thirteen

I HELD THE DOOR to the dining room open for Dawn. Kate stood at the door opposite, guiding her guests to their tables. Edlynn waved me over.

"I think I'm on the table next to you," Dawn said as I followed her over to our seats.

"I swapped your seat, Dawn," Ailsa said. "So you're nearer to us. Nobody will notice."

A raucous laugh filled the dining room. "That's Ellie's boyfriend, Ben," Dawn said. "Kate's sister ..."

We watched him pick Ellie up and spin her around as she bashfully tapped on his shoulder with her clutch bag to put her down.

"Maybe a strong coffee should be the first thing he orders," Ailsa said with a raised eyebrow.

"Oh, Ailsa," Edlynn said. "It's young love. I think it's beautiful."

The turning paddle on the boat slowed, and the steamer came to a halt in a small inlet on the river.

Dawn chatted to a young couple seated at her table before turning her chair slightly to speak with us.

"What a lovely spot to stop for dinner," Edlynn said.

One side of the inlet had cliff faces, the other filled its banks with rocks and wildflowers. A small sandy riverbank met a path leading up the hillside to a hilltop café filled with diners on the balcony. We took in the view, and within a few minutes, the captain and his wife joined Kate's table as we looked over our menus.

The menu wasn't as exotic as I had imagined from my conversation with Amie. Maybe she was prone to a little exaggeration. It looked like good hearty country food to me. Dawn would be in her element. I ordered a leek and potato soup, and cider and honey drunken chicken, with a banoffee pie for dessert.

"I don't know why banoffee pie always feels like such a treat," I said.

"It is so easy to make," Ailsa said. "A pie base filled with *Dulce de Leche*, covered in sliced bananas and topped with whipped cream and grated chocolate. Anyone can whip one up in no time."

I placed my napkin across my knee. "I don't know why we don't eat it more often."

"*Because* it's a treat," Edlynn said.

We all devoured our food, and Edlynn even broke her tea drinking tradition by indulging in an after-dinner coffee. Dawn had joined us at our table, and the now familiar sounds of the paddle steamer started again as we prepared to head back to land. The jazz band started playing louder, and the dance floor filled. I gave up on trying to convince Ailsa for a dance, but Edlynn and Dawn were the perfect dance partners, and Ailsa said she was happy to watch our bags.

After kicking up my heels for a few songs, I walked out to get some fresh air, passing Amie as she helped a waitress pack Kate's gifts into neat bags, ready for the journey back to Folly Gate. I stopped for a moment to peek through a green door with a small porthole window in it. The engine room door hid the whirring and hissing of the swinging dials of the engine's gauges and valves, and green, red, blue and yellow pipes weaved their way around the room. I snapped my head back when I saw Kate's sister and her boyfriend giggling and heading straight for the door.

The door flung open. "Oops, we've been caught," Ben said.

"Oh, shush." Ellie giggled.

"Your secret is safe with me," I said with jocular disapproval.

"Thank you," she said and grabbed Ben's hand, dragging him back to the party.

As I walked back to the deck, the market-town lights of Totnes came into view. I stopped to admire the twinkling lights of the town before returning inside to look for my friends. Ailsa was waiting and ready to head home. Edlynn and Dawn chatted with Kate.

"It has been a wonderful night, Kate," Edlynn said. "Thank you so much for inviting us."

"You're welcome, and I'm glad you've enjoyed yourselves. When we get back, the coach is waiting to take us back to Folly Gate. We're going to stop at The Cidered Apple for an after party. You're welcome to join us there too, if you like."

I noticed Amie sitting on a bench at the edge of the room, dropping more of her remedies under her tongue, and walked over to see if she was okay.

"It seems I like the water even less than I thought," she said when I asked after her.

"Well, we're almost back to Totnes," I said and took a seat next to her.

"I think he's going to need more than a coffee," Amie said.

I looked across to see Ben sitting, or rather swaying, and lifting a bottle of prosecco to his lips, as Ellie tried to convince him to put it down. She managed to pry it from his hands but he knocked it off the table, spilling its contents *and* his coffee across the floor.

"He's always been like that," Amie said. "He's all fun and games, but doesn't know when to stop."

"Sounds like it's not the first time you have seen him like this," I said.

"No," Amie said casually. "We used to date in university. Doesn't look like much has changed. I hope Ellie is up to it. She seems to think so – she's engaged to him."

"Well, there's a lid for every pot, they say."

Amie laughed half-heartedly.

The paddle steamer slowed for the last time, and we collected our belongings and headed towards the gangway. The crew sent us off with a fond farewell, and Andrew, the cocktail waiter, stood in place of the captain.

"Good night, ladies," he said as we disembarked.

"Thank you for the cocktails," Edlynn giggled.

Ailsa nodded politely.

But my concern wasn't with farewells or where the captain might be ... my concern laid firmly on the stony stares of the crew.

We made it back to Folly Gate after Kate's party and decided not to join them at The Cidered Apple. John was there to welcome them to his pub when they arrived and didn't seem bothered about the *motley crew*. I walked with Edlynn and Ailsa up Archer Street until I turned left to go home, and they continued up together to their homes.

I kicked off my shoes and slunk onto the sofa.

"Looks like you had a good night," Jasper's voice came from my aunt's chair.

I sat up. "It was ... thanks. I think I'm ready for my bed, though."

Jasper jumped off the chair and joined me on the sofa.

"Nothing exciting going on here?" I asked, as he rubbed his face into my palm.

"No, very quiet. Our houseguests are asleep, and I can sleep easier knowing the locks are secure."

"*Ah,* sleep … that sounds good. Are you hungry, Jasper? Do you want a snack?"

"No, thanks. I found a few snacks today."

"I don't want to know," I said, as Jasper curled up and rested his chin on my lap. "It's so quiet here at night. It almost feels like you have to tiptoe around in case you disturb the peace."

"That's contentment, Daisy," he said as he closed his eyes.

The sound of my ringing phone snapped us out of our quiet moment. "Who's ringing at this time of night?" I said as I sat up and fumbled through my bag for my phone.

"Ethan? Is everything okay?" I asked.

"Sorry to ring so late, Daisy, but I could use your help."

"Oh, what is it?"

"You've been at Kate's party?" he asked.

"Yes, I've just got in. Has something happened? Everyone got back to Folly Gate on the bus."

"I've had a call come through … about the captain."

"The captain?" My mind went back to the faces of the crew and the fact that he hadn't seen us off. "What is it?"

"Unfortunately, he's dead."

"But he seemed all right at dinner … I don't understand."

"I have to get down there and I think your expertise might help. You said you've been studying gardening and herbs or whatever it is you do with Ailsa …"

"Yes, I didn't know you had noticed."

"*Well* ... your garden is starting to look really well put together," he said sheepishly.

"Oh, thank you." I smiled for a moment.

"Anyway, what was I saying?" he said, collecting his thoughts. "It is only an initial assessment, but someone has said it looks like he may have been poisoned. We'll need to investigate further. The ambulance tried to treat him for hemlock poisoning. But unfortunately, he didn't make it."

"Hemlock poisoning? The quail ..." I said, without missing a beat.

"Quail?" Ethan asked.

"I thought it was a strange thing to put on the menu. It stood out to me. The food on the rest of the menu was quite traditional."

"But what has quail got to do with hemlock? Daisy ... Daisy?"

"Come and pick me up. I'll explain on the way."

After returning from Totnes for the second time in the same night, I knocked quietly on Ailsa's front door. I could only imagine what she would be like having her sleep disturbed. But when she heard what I had to tell her, I was sure she wouldn't mind. The sound of her heavy footsteps pounded down her hallway and I held my breath.

"I'm not sure this is one of your best ideas, Daisy," Jasper said. "You should have at least called first ..."

"They never do ..." I said.

"True, true," he replied.

The heavy cottage door opened to Ailsa standing there in her robe, its frayed edges matching her hair which she had tied off in sections with torn rags. She must have worn that robe for years.

"Daisy, what are you doing here? It's five in the morning."

"I'm sorry, but I needed to speak with you," I said.

She caught me looking down at her tartan slippers with tiny little bag-pipes attached at the front.

"They were a gift," she said. "And they do the job. It would be a shame to throw them out."

I pursed my lips together, stifling a giggle. Our Ailsa was quite the enigma. She huffed at me like I was impossible, but she was quite the sight. "Well, come in then. You're always dilly dallying. I'll put the kettle on. *And* you can stop staring at my hair. I'm trying something new, that's all."

"I'm sure it will look lovely. You could always—"

"Uh," Ailsa held her hand up for me to stop. "That will be enough, thank you."

Jasper followed me into Ailsa's kitchen. "She's cranky in the morning," he said.

"Don't," I said as Ailsa looked directly at him. Jasper had an ability to give me the childish giggles and I could feel them rising in me. I was there on a serious case matter and had to pull myself together ... act *professional*.

"I'll be back in a minute," she said.

I pulled down the tea caddy, set it on the table and tempered the teapot. It wasn't long before she returned, with her hair perfectly straightened, dressed and ready for the day. I said nothing, but it seemed like there were some things from the non-magic world that still intrigued her. However, not enough to stop her from pulling out her wand when she needed a *quick dress* spell.

"I told you some things were not worth giving up for magic," I said. "Like hot showers and—"

"What is so important you had to wake me?" Ailsa asked as she poured the tea.

"I need your help."

I explained to her about the captain and how Ethan was already working on recalling any quail from the supplier for Kate's party.

"The hemlock must have come from the quail," I said. "Ethan and the Sarge are putting it down to food poisoning. The captain had alcohol in his system, and because of the state of his health, they said it was a cocktail for disaster."

Ailsa added sugar to her English Breakfast tea and placed her teaspoon on her saucer. "You're right about the quail, Daisy. It is entirely possible the hemlock could have been passed through the quail. Quail eat hemlock seeds but have developed an immunity to the toxins."

"Yes, I remember it from my studies," I said.

"This is why it is so important to learn about the old ways, and not to always take shortcuts with our wands."

I listened. "So, what do you think? A simple food poisoning?"

"I would agree. Quail can be poisonous during their migration, but only on certain routes. It is entirely possible ... especially if others were ill from the party. But there is one flaw with your theory ..."

"There is? What's that?" I asked.

"It is not autumn, Daisy ... and *we* are not in Africa," – she sipped her tea – "which means ... the hemlock had to have come from somewhere else."

CHAPTER FOURTEEN

T HE MORNING TWILIGHT WAS lifting as I made my way through the familiar streets of Folly Gate. I walked on the balls of my feet, not wanting the sounds of my boots to disturb the stillness. I slowly opened the small wrought-iron gate to Ethan's front garden. After looking around on the ground, I found a small pebble stone and tossed it gently up to the second-storey window ... but there was no response. I tried again ... nothing.

"You could always try the door ..." Jasper said with a glimmer of sarcasm.

I looked around for another stone, but before I could toss it, I heard the window being pushed open and Ethan's whispered voice, "Daisy? I thought you were going to get some sleep. Wait there."

I walked with Jasper to the front door, watching the lights turn on and off as he made his way downstairs.

Ethan squinted through the open doorway at us. "My doorbell works, you know," he said.

Jasper meowed.

"What is it?"

"Can we come in?" I asked.

"Yes, yes. Go through to the kitchen." He closed the door behind us and followed us through, before going to the fridge, drinking straight from the milk carton and flicking on the kitchen light. "Umm ..." He looked around the kitchen, the milk carton still in his hand. "Do you want some tea?"

"No thanks," I said. "I've just had some at Ailsa's."

"You were at Ailsa's?"

"She was about as pleased as you are to see me, but I didn't think it could wait."

"Okay ..."

"You said to me on the way back to Folly Gate you were ordering a recall on the quail, because I told you that quails have developed an immunity to hemlock, and it could have come from there ..."

"Right," he said.

"Well ... I might be wrong."

"What do you mean?" he asked, as he returned the milk to the fridge.

"I'm right about the migratory quail eating the hemlock seeds ... but they only do this in the autumn."

"Right," he said. "And?"

"Well, I don't see any fallen leaves around Folly Gate ..."

"Oh, right ... Oh ... ooohhh. We're in spring."

"That's right, making it highly unlikely a decent enough amount of hemlock would occur in the spring. And not to mention, they are usually only poisonous on their return to Africa from Europe ..."

"Well, I'll have to remember to stay away from the quail in the autumn."

"I'm sure you'll manage," I said.

"You think the hemlock may have come from another source?"

"That's exactly what I think."

Ethan scratched his unkempt hair. "We have to check into this, Daisy. Let me get dressed. We'll visit the Sarge."

I waited in the kitchen with Jasper, remembering his mum serving us afternoon teas at the same small table, as children on Saturdays. The cupboards still looked the same, except the hand painted cupboards were now chipped. And the floral dusky rose wallpaper had turned down at its edges. The large kitchen window looked out over the sink to the woods, and the garden his parents had taken so much pride in had withered and begun to moss over. A house filled with photographs of happier times and knick-knacks collected over a lifetime ... now felt so empty.

"Ready?" Ethan's voice came from the hallway. "The Sarge is up pretty early. We might be in luck and not have to wake him."

We followed Ethan out to his neat Vauxhall sedan. "It's open," he said. "Jasper? Coming for a ride?" He held his door open for him to jump through to the back, and we headed off to the Sarge's house.

"Out of curiosity ..." Ethan asked me. "How did you know which window was mine?"

"I took a chance. Your model car collection sat in the window in exactly the same place I remembered, so I figured more likely than not ... not much else would have changed."

"You're right ... not much has. I can't bring myself to ... yet."

"Oh, I know how that feels. It took me a while to make Aunt Olivia's house my own."

"My problem is I'm not sure I want to make that house my own."

"I understand," I said. "How are things with your parents? You never really speak about them."

"There's not much to tell. Nothing has changed. But Dad insists on being near Mum. I don't know that I would be any different if I found myself in that position. It was costing him a small fortune to stay closer to her, so I sold my flat and ... well, he is closer now. I thought he might come back to the house at some point, but he has said there is nothing to come home to, and I find myself in a sort of limbo ... not wanting to sell their house, but also wanting to live my life. But it suits me for now. And I still visit her whenever I can."

"I'm sorry, Ethan. It must be difficult."

"Well, she has some of the best doctors around, and all we can do is take one day at a time."

Ethan's tyres hit the gravel of the Sarge's drive. As we pulled up, we saw the Sarge stand up from his conservatory table and motion for us to go around to the front door. He greeted us holding a half-eaten bacon bap. He pushed down on the base, which was wrapped in folded down waxed paper, and took a bite.

"DC Fairfield," he said through a mouthful of bacon, "and Daisy ..."

"Apologies for the early call, Sarge," Ethan began. "But we have some information ... well, Daisy has some information that we thought should come to you as soon as possible."

The Sarge screwed up the empty waxed paper.

Ethan continued, "We have reason to believe the hemlock may have come from another source ... not the quail, as first suspected."

"Well, you better come in then," he said, as he ushered us through to the conservatory.

I was busy explaining to the Sarge about the migratory habits of quail and their love of hemlock seeds when a voice came from the conservatory door, "Daisy?"

I recognised the woman from my shop. "Mrs Watts."

"Oh, you remembered," she said. "This is the nice lady that helped me pick the candle—"

The Sarge interrupted, "I am well acquainted with Ms Daisy Banks, Mother."

"Oh, lovely," she said before placing a plate with four neatly wrapped baps on the table. "Help yourself. Bacon and ketchup. There's plenty more."

Ethan reached over and passed me one. "Thank you," I said.

Mrs Watts stood at the table for a moment. "Are you working together again, Daisy?"

The Sarge breathed in impatiently. "This is official police business, Mother."

"Oh, so you *are* working together again," she said. "You were a lot of help in the last case, so I've heard."

Ethan took his chance, "And I could use Daisy's expertise on this."

The Sarge took another bap from the plate and unwrapped it. He leant back into his chair and looked at the ceiling as he chewed on a mouthful, deep in thought. "The toxicology report will not be back for a couple of days ... If we could get ahead of that ... And Daisy does seem to know what she's talking about ..." He looked across at me before slapping his hand on the table. "Right, you two ... get to work ... off you go, before I change my mind."

Ethan kept his car running when he pulled up outside my house. "Try to get some sleep, Daisy, and we'll catch up when we have any new information for each other."

"Thanks. It's been a long night," I said, as I unbuckled my seatbelt.

He smiled. "It's good to have you back on the job, too," he said to Jasper as he made his way out the open door.

I closed the door and turned to the house. The curtains were open, which meant my houseguests were probably awake. Scarlet opened the door. "Daisy ... we've been waiting for you. Edlynn and Ailsa are here too."

I didn't hear Edlynn approach as I untied my laces. Maybe she was feeling more comfortable around my shadow friends. You don't float around in front of everybody, you know. It's quite a personal thing to do.

"I came as soon as I heard from Kate," Edlynn said. "She's been calling everyone who went last night to make sure no one else is ill. She asked if we could put a basket together for the captain's wife – to send condolences. I called into Ailsa's on the way ..."

"We'll make a basket for her as soon as we open the shop," I said.

"When she said she couldn't get a hold of you ..." Edlynn continued.

"I was with Ethan," I said.

"Ethan?"

"There might be more to this poisoning than we think," I said.

"Well, I'll make a fresh pot of Earl Grey, and you can tell us all about it."

I came in to find Amber, Em and Ailsa chatting over breakfast. Edlynn had obviously been working her magic again as she had laid the table with everything you could want for breakfast. Croissants, fresh sliced fruit, crispy bacon ... and if something wasn't there, I was sure she would be happy to *wand* it up. Unfortunately for shadow witches, our cooking doesn't particularly appeal to other witches. We can do it – but it takes a lot of effort. I have both delighted and disappointed as I've been training. It's a lot safer to make everything from scratch if we are hosting a *witchy brunch*. Wanded up shadow food will leave a nasty taste in the mouth of an unassuming witch.

After a brief fussing over, Jasper ate some mackerel, made his way to his cushions at the end of the table and curled into them to catch up on some sleep, after following me around all morning.

"I really think you should get some sleep, Daisy," Ailsa said. "We'll wait here and wake you if we hear anything from Ethan. What is Ethan doing on this case, anyway? Surely, they could have called in someone from Plymouth or Exeter? They have a bigger police force there."

"He told me a friend had called in a favour," I said. "And he thought I might be able to help. I hope he's right because something doesn't sit right with me. Hemlock coming out of nowhere ... the crossover potion *and* the follies being destroyed. The timing seems all a little too coincidental."

"You think it's a witch?" Edlynn asked. "What witches would Kate know?"

"Well, she knows us ..." Ailsa said.

Edlynn shook her head, a little embarrassed. "Oh, goodness. Of course. But it wasn't us. And what kind of witch would have business with a captain?"

Amber refilled her tea. "We didn't find out anything new at the Gathering. Nobody seems to know a thing about the follies. And there were witches from all over the country. Thankfully, we all had a good time, and the party went well into the next day."

Scarlet sat down at the table and buttered a breakfast muffin. "I think it might be a stretch to suggest the two incidents are related."

"You do?" I asked.

"Witches aren't the only ones who can get their hands on hemlock," she said.

"That's true," I said.

Em dipped a *soldier* into her soft-boiled egg. "If I didn't know any better, I would think there is a rogue witch around – using magic that is way above her level."

"Maybe," Amber said. "None of the covens seem to know anything. But how could an ordinary witch get hold of a crossover potion? Maybe it's an alchemist trying to use magic."

I stood up from the table. "Well, whoever it is, I need to find out as quickly as I can. Gwendolyn has her suspicions about me, and I need to prove to her I have nothing to do with it. I didn't ask to be given access to the follies. In fact, I hardly know how I should use them, except to move around quickly. We need to cover all possibilities. If it *is* a rogue witch, then we have to flush her out. And if the captain died of a simple, yet disastrous, food poisoning incident, then we won't lose anything by looking for her, anyway. Maybe it's time Folly Gate had a good clear out – a stocktake of sorts. We are the only coven in this area, and *we* should know *everything* that is happening in it."

"You're right," Ailsa said.

"Can you imagine if there is a rogue witch in Folly Gate," – Edlynn sipped her tea – "and our coven let her slip through our fingers? Not on my wand. I agree with Daisy. We'll flush them out. Do you have a plan?"

Jasper lifted his head and opened one eye.

"Actually, I do," I said. "And you're going to help me."

Chapter Fifteen

T HE NEXT MORNING, I was well rested but had heard nothing from Ethan. I headed to *Liv's Lumières*, but not before following the trail of fresh baked goods filling the air. Home Sweet Scone is not a place to visit when you're hungry ... but it is *also,* most definitely, the place to go to when you're hungry ... especially when you've skipped breakfast.

"First customer of the day," Baxter greeted me.

"Morning, Baxter," I replied. "I have come for breakfast ... but also, I'd like to enter the Folly Gate Cake Off."

"I didn't know you baked, Daisy."

"I've had a little more time since I moved to Folly Gate," I said. "And I thought I'd try to get more into the spirit of the town."

"That's good to hear." He smiled as he passed me a piece of paper. "You need to fill in your details here and what you would like to enter, and take the form to Penelope Black at the council offices. She's been in charge of the competition for years. There are other competitions going on for the festival, if anyone else you know wants to enter. Here, take some of these entry forms. I know Ailsa's cooking is nothing to be sneezed at."

"Thank you," I said and slipped the papers into my bag.

Baxter picked up his notepad and pen. "Now, what can I get you for breakfast?"

"What's your special today?"

"Well, you could always have our full English breakfast ... but I *have* made a delicious *kedgeree* this morning. The smoked haddock is from Carter's Fishmongers and the eggs are fresh off the Paget farm."

"Sounds delicious," I said.

"One kedgeree coming up ..." He peered out the front window. "And I see Jasper has followed you."

"He has a tendency to ..."

"Well, sneak him through to the courtyard. I'll bring your breakfast out there. I don't think I could stare at those sad eyes while you sat eating." He laughed and gave a little wink.

I made my way through the cafe with Jasper in tow and found a corner table where he could curl up under my feet.

"I'll get you something if you like, Jasper," I said to him as he found a comfortable spot.

"I'm okay," he said. "I'd rather hear what you're up to. Why would you want to enter a baking competition all of a sudden? I mean, you'll be up against the best in Folly Gate ... we have some fine bakers in town. And also, something else you might not have considered ... Jenifer Penton has been the head judge for the last eight years. After that case on her estate, I think you would be hard pressed to get her to award you a ribbon."

"I'm not concerned with winning," I said. "*This time,* participating is the most important thing."

"Well, you won't get a ribbon for that either," Jasper said.

"One kedgeree for Daisy," Baxter's voice came into the courtyard. He placed the warm bowl gently in front of me. "And a little something for Jasper." He set a small bowl in front of him, to which Jasper sat up straight away. "Fresh chicken livers ... I hope he likes it. Apparently, it's like catnip to them."

I finished my breakfast and walked along the Folly Gate High Street with my competition entry filled out, ready to drop at the council offices, when I heard a car pull up beside me. With the High Street being pedestrianised, after a *very unfortunate incident*, it could only be one person.

"I've been looking all over for you," Ethan said through his opened window.

"I just had breakfast—"

"The Sarge called," he said. "They found traces of hemlock in the prosecco."

"The ones I gave Kate for her birthday? I gave her six bottles. I'll have to call Cara. She can't be selling them to her customers—"

"Your friend's prosecco was at the party? Well, any prosecco that *wasn't* at the party might not be affected, but I would hold off opening any more bottles until we're certain. It looks like someone may have deliberately added the hemlock. We haven't found it in all the bottles, though. They're testing the rest of the prosecco from the party now. Can you get a bottle of your friend's prosecco to me ... maybe a few? Just to be sure."

"Of course."

"Good. I'm checking in on guests from the party. There's a couple of them I would like to check on again ... and I need to pick up a list of suppliers the paddle steamer has used in the last six months. The captain's wife said she would have them ready for me."

"Well, I could do that," I said. "I'm delivering a bereavement basket to her this morning. Kate asked Edlynn if we could put one together when they spoke yesterday."

"Okay. Well, that will work. I'll call Mrs Garbis and let her know to expect you. Oh, you'll have to take these directions." He handed me a small hand-drawn map. "Following a *sat-nav* doesn't always work out of town." Ethan released his handbrake. "Maybe you were right, Daisy. Autumnal quail ..." – he shrugged – "who knew?"

He continued on up the street, receiving a few friendly waves from business owners opening up for the day.

"I won't be a minute, Jasper," I said, as we arrived at the council offices.

A friendly smile greeted me at reception, and I handed over my entry.

"You've just made it," the receptionist said. "Entries close at 3pm today."

I smiled back at her. "I'm looking forward to it."

"Good luck," she said, as I made my way towards the door.

I stopped in my tracks and turned to her. "Thank you," I said, before continuing out the door. "Luck is the last thing a witch needs," I said under my breath. "Let's go, Jasper. We're in."

"You're very *cloak and dagger* today, Daisy," he said. "I don't mind it. I kind of like it, in fact. But I *would* like to know what it is that we're *into*."

I picked him up and carried on walking. "We have to keep this to ourselves for now, Jasper. But we're *into* ... shadow cakes."

"Well," he said. "I can unequivocally tell you I am most certainly *not* ... into shadow cakes."

"I know that. I am going to enter one in the competition."

"Aaah, then you'll most likely win. I get it."

"I told you at breakfast ... *winning* is not the goal."

"Then what is it?"

"We said we were going to flush out the rogue witch. And that's what we will do – with a little help from Morton's tools ..."

"Alchemists' tools will attract witches ..."

"Exactly. Then all there is left for me to do is sit back and see who can't get enough of my cake ... but more importantly ... *who* simply can't swallow it."

CHAPTER SIXTEEN

EDLYNN TIED OFF THE last bow on the basket and snipped the ends into perfect triangles. "There you are," she said. "Now, drive slowly on those back roads. The high hedges don't leave a lot of room for mistakes. And I'll see you back for morning tea."

The new delivery van had seen little use since I bought it, but I tried to show it around when I could. Mostly it had sat idle, parked behind the shop. I hoped to see it out on the road more, as our delivery service grew.

Jasper kept me company while I drove about ten minutes out of town. I came off a main road and followed a winding country lane, looking left and right for a sign to Swallowfield Village. Ethan's map said not to follow the *sat-nav*, as you would end up in the middle of a field. Instead, I was to follow the lane down until I came across a red telephone box with a bus shelter to the right, then turn left, follow the road over a small stream, keep going past a white cottage and take a quick left up the hill.

"That must be it," I said to Jasper. "Now keep yourself out of sight and don't wander far. I don't want to be caught out having to call my cat back."

"Understood," he said. "I'll just stretch my legs. I promise."

"No sneaking about ..."

"No sneaking ..." he said. "Understood."

I pulled up the handbrake and opened my door, letting Jasper slip over my lap and disappear into the woodland on the side of the drive. It was a modest house, but its positioning on the hillside hinted it had a large acreage attached. I closed the van door, straightened my hair and knocked on the front door of the house, basket in hand. I didn't have to wait long for a familiar face to answer the door – although this time her face was tear stained and much paler than I remembered from the party.

"Daisy Banks? I remember you from the party." She took a bite from her apple and observed me. "I didn't know you were a policewoman. You don't look the type," she said through her mouthful of apple.

"Well, I'm not actually. I am consulted when needed. But today I am working a little for both of my jobs. My shop has a delivery for your family, and I also need to pick up some papers from your mother." I waited for her to invite me in but instead found myself filling in the silence, "I want to pass on my deepest condolences—"

"Thanks," she said. "Mum's in the garden. I'll take you through."

I carried the basket through a large conservatory at the back of the house. Its windows gave a clear view across the fields and down to the river. Someone had re-purposed a large ship's steering wheel into a chandelier and hung it high from the ceiling.

The young woman pointed her apple towards the garden. "She's down there." And before I could say anything, she closed the sliding door and went back into the house.

I stepped out onto a long balcony and could see a woman sitting at a table with a pot of tea and a book in her hand. I picked up a fallen silk scarf and placed it on the small garden table before heading down to Mrs Gabris.

The pebbled path sloped downwards, leading into a secret garden. An ivy-covered stone archway with a wooden gate sat at the base of the path. A quiet place to be. So quiet, in fact, that Mrs Gabris heard my approach and turned to me before closing her book.

"It's one of yours," she said. "I like to support local artists. It was on sale at the Penton bookshop. And when DC Fairfield called and said you would come … well, you know what it's like in times like this – you think everything is a *sign*."

"Well, I will have to thank Jenifer," I said. "I didn't know she was stocking my books. *In a Manor of Steeping*. Not my best work, I have to say. The reviews weren't very kind … not enough *tea*, apparently."

"Well, I'm trying to take my mind off things, as you can imagine. And speaking of tea … would you like one?"

"If it's no bother," I said.

"No bother at all," she said as she picked up her phone and pressed it to her ear. "Rosaleen, can you bring down an extra teacup, please … for our visitor?"

I placed the gift basket on the table. "A gift from Kate," I said. "The host of Saturday night's party. She wanted to pass on her deepest condolences … as do we."

She offered me a seat. "I have the list ready for you. I hope it is of some help. Albert usually took care of those matters. I only recently had access to the business paperwork."

"Thank you, Mrs Gabris—"

"Please call me Lyla. Albert seemed to have everything under control. So it has been quite a feat finding my way around it all." She paused and breathed out deeply. "I had always trusted him, Daisy. But, you know … when you've been married for so long, you're bound to have arguments … We have always taken care of different parts of the business. I took care of the bookings and staffing … that sort of thing. And he took care of everything else."

"I understand," I replied.

Lyla shifted uncomfortably in her chair. "You're working with the police? DC Fairfield said you are a trusted colleague of the Folly Gate constabulary."

"Well, that is nice to hear. I'm consulting for them. But if there's something you want to tell me ... or something you would like us to look into."

"Well, I'm trying to be as helpful as I can. A lot I could tell you would be inconsequential ... But ... well, I don't know. It could be nothing. But a few weeks ago ... I was with Albert – in the captain's office on the steamer – when an alarm set off. An engineer radioed through and said there was a problem in the engine room. It must have been quite urgent because Albert left without closing his safe properly."

"I see. And you saw something?" I asked.

"I did," her voice lowered. "Thousands of pounds, stacked neatly at the back of the safe. When I asked him about it, he was so casual. 'It's for some suppliers,' he said. But when I questioned him further, asking why he didn't write them a cheque or pay with a bank transfer, he got angry. And that's when he said I could look through the books if I didn't believe him. But to be honest, I didn't even know what I was looking at ... and he wasn't interested in explaining it to me. There is still some debt attached to the steamer but I'm sure the insurance will sort that out."

"Do you think your husband was having issues with anyone ... or maybe with finances?"

"Issues? Albert had issues with just about everyone, including his family. But they were only usual everyday problems. Certainly nothing overly concerning."

"I understand. Well, I'll pass it on. And if you think of anything at all, call DC Fairfield. Any information could help."

She looked at me, quite confused. "Is there something I should know? Something you're not telling me?"

I drew in a breath. "No," I lied. "But I know the police in Folly Gate will give you all the answers you need as they have them. I am only here to deliver a gift and pick up the list of suppliers."

Rosaleen arrived at the table, interrupting our conversation. She placed an empty teacup and saucer in front of me and an unopened packet of custard creams.

"Oh, Rosaleen," Lyla said. "You could have at least ... oh, never mind. Thank you."

Rosaleen paused for a moment and looked at her mother before looking back at me and turning on her heel to walk back to the house.

"I'm sorry," Lyla said. "She's not taking it well. The last time she spoke with her father they argued ... and nobody wants an argument to be the last conversation they had with someone they love."

"That must be difficult for her," I said. "And what about you, Lyla?"

"Like I said, we had our ups and downs, as any marriage does, but we have ... *had* known each other since childhood. I always imagined we would somehow face death together, you know, holding hands ... telling each other 'I love you' ... not suffocating to death on a galley floor." She burst into tears.

I looked up towards the house as she took a tissue from a sleeve and wiped her nose. Rosaleen stood at a window looking out at us as she spoke on her phone.

Lyla sniffed and looked up at the house. "They're so secretive, aren't they? Were we that secretive at that age? Since she has come back from university, she is so private. I never see her friends, and she's always away at festivals or parties and never lets me know what she's been doing. I think she has a new boyfriend at the moment, though. She always seems to be on her phone, chatting and texting. Now I know what my mother had to put up with." She gave a delicate chuckle before turning her attention back to me.

"What is she studying?" I asked.

"She is reading Law. But she took a year off and came back to help on the steamer. She never told me why she wanted to take a year off, but I was glad to have her around. I think she worries about life a little too much. But Albert always made sure there was enough to take care of her, even if anything should happen to him. She has nothing to worry about."

"I see," I said. "And do you have family around?"

"Yes, my sister is coming down from Yorkshire today. She should be here this afternoon."

"That's good to hear …" I stood up from my chair. "I won't keep you any longer."

"Thank you, Daisy," she said as she passed me an envelope. "The suppliers … Oh, and thank you for the basket. It's a very sweet gesture. You can make your way out around the side of the house, if you don't mind. I think I'm going to sit here a little while longer."

CHAPTER SEVENTEEN

I DROVE STRAIGHT TO the police station to give Ethan the list of suppliers and fill him in on my discussion with Lyla. Jasper let himself out when we arrived and disappeared down an alley. The constabulary was empty, except for the Sarge, who waved me into his office before I could ring the bell.

"Morning ..." He looked at his watch. "Afternoon, I should say."

He continued eating his two rounds of white bread sandwiches. A blue lunchbox sat open next to him with a green apple and a packet of crisps. At least he had been spared a juice box, which had been replaced with a small bottle of 100% orange juice ... with *no bits*.

"It looks like you're being well looked after, Sarge," I said.

He chuckled. "My mother's only here for a few days ... and she insisted. No doubt she'll check it when I get home to make sure I ate it all." He waved off a laugh. "Are you looking for Ethan? He's on his way back here. You're welcome to wait." He offered me half of his sandwich.

"No, thank you," I said. "I told Edlynn I'd pick us up some lunch."

He gestured towards reception. "You're in luck. Fairfield's coming in now."

What is it with people's reliance on *luck*? I thought to myself.

Ethan tossed some papers on his desk and walked into the office, wearing a smart navy suit, collared white shirt and tie. "Afternoon," he said, as he eyed the Sarge's lunch.

"Help yourself," he said. "Cheese and piccalilli ... I couldn't eat another thing."

"Thanks, Sarge." Ethan took the last half of the sandwich and bit into it. "That's a good sandwich," he said through a mouthful.

The Sarge looked pleased.

I reached into my bag and passed Ethan the envelope from Mrs Garbis. "The list of suppliers."

"Thanks," he said and tucked it under his arm. "Are you busy now, Daisy? I'm heading up to the Folly View Hotel. We could see if there's anything else we need to follow up."

"Sure," I said. "I just need to give Edlynn a call."

I followed Ethan as he added the envelope to a growing stack of papers on his desk. "It hasn't been that high in a while," he said, as he grabbed his coat. "After you ..."

We made our way out of the station and towards his car. "Love the new van, Daisy. Your signage looks like Goran's work?"

"It is. There's not much he can't do in his shop. It looks like *you* have a new car, too."

"It's a constabulary car. I don't have to be in uniform as much as I used to be."

"Moving up in the ranks?"

"Something like that." He smiled.

I relayed everything Mrs Gabris had said to me as we drove to the Folly View Hotel. Many of Kate's guests were staying at the hotel, and Ethan wanted to get as much information as he could before they left. The grand hotel, with its marble and mirrors and black with gold detailing, was a popular place in its heyday. And it had continued to hold its reputation for high paying guests and events. I suspect it may have been the inspiration for Kate's party, keeping the guests in the same theme for the entire weekend.

A smartly dressed woman, with her hair tied back in a neat low bun, greeted us, "Welcome to Folly View Hotel."

"Good afternoon," Ethan said. "We would like to speak with some of your guests."

"Some of our guests?" she asked with a corporate smile. "Are they expecting you?"

Ethan showed her his identification.

"I understand, Detective," she said. "Would you like me to arrange a private room for you? We have offices in the back of the hotel ..." She kept her smile.

"Thank you, but these guests are in the Penthouse Suite. There is enough privacy there," he replied.

I turned to take in the well-maintained art deco architecture when Jasper caught my eye. He sat on the stone wall of the steps, with his face lifting to catch the sun. I was getting used to him turning up unexpectedly, not knowing where he had come from. But then, even a witch's *familiar* should have business that is solely their own.

I turned back to Ethan as the receptionist slid him an entry card. "I can have someone escort you if you like," she offered.

"Not necessary," Ethan said. "I've been here before."

"Well ... then welcome back, Detective. And if you need anything, let me know."

Ethan slid the entry card into the panel of the gold elevators and pressed 'P'.

"Doesn't look like Ellie has spared any expense either," I said.

We waited in the low hum and clanging of the old elevator until the doors opened. Ellie stood in a hotel robe in the small foyer that opened out into the suite. "Daisy? Oh, I was expecting room service. I've ordered something up for Ben. He's still nursing quite the hangover. Detective ... Come in." Ellie sat down at a small linen-covered window table. "What a terrible end to the evening," she continued. "We were all having such a good time ... and we had no idea something so awful was happening."

"I can understand the shock," Ethan said. "We wanted to stop by and see if Ben is feeling any better than yesterday. If he isn't, we would like to advise him to visit the hospital ... as a precaution."

"It's just a hangover, I'm sure," Ellie said. "But if you insist ..."

We heard the toilet flush, and Ben staggered out of the bathroom, his hair wild and his face pale. "Partied a little too hard," he laughed as he ran his fingers through his hair. "Nothing seems to make it feel better." He tossed a packet of pills across the bar, picked up a small dark bottle and took a large gulp of the liquid. "I'll try anything at this point," he said, as he rested his hands against the bar before searching through the suite's small bar for something to quench his thirst. "I'm sure a few more glasses of this and I'll be feeling better," he said as he poured a large glass of orange juice.

"Well, just to be on the safe side, we want you to visit the hospital," Ethan said. "This is my card. If you could let me know that you're feeling better and have the all clear from the hospital ..."

"It's just a hangover. But fine," he said. "If there's nothing else ... I'm going to lie down."

"There is just one other thing," I said, before he left the room. "Can I ask you what you had for dinner?"

"Let me see." Ben squinted as he tried to remember. "Oh, I remember ... chicken. Yes, that's what I had. A perfectly cooked little chicken. The captain loved it too – ate the bones and all. Said it was the way to eat them. Not my cup of tea, but each to their own."

"And what about to drink?" I asked.

"Oh … well." He laughed. "I couldn't say … it's all a bit of a blur, to be honest. Cocktails … Lager … I'm sure someone passed around some shots."

"Well, you have DC Fairfield's card if you remember anything else," I said.

"You seem pretty concerned over a food poisoning—" Ben began.

Ethan cut him off, "Your wellbeing is our only concern at the moment, Ben. So … if you could … just get yourself to the hospital."

<hr/>

We returned the card to reception and headed back across the lobby.

"It seems Ben is the only other sick guest," Ethan said. "And it may only be a hangover, but hopefully we'll hear from him soon and put our minds at rest."

"Maybe it *is* the quail," I said. "An unfortunate bout of food poisoning … But I think we should check out a few other leads."

"Well, I'm going to leave the recall of the quail in place until we know what is happening for sure."

"I was thinking more about the captain's wife and her daughter. I think there is more going on than they are letting on. Rosaleen seemed rather unaffected by her father's death … but her mother said she wasn't taking it well …"

"We all grieve differently, Dais'," he said.

"I know. It's just that Lyla said to me there were debts on the boat, but she assumed the insurance would take care of it. But *you* said you did the financial check on the boat loan, and the loan company told you everything was in order. I am wondering if he didn't take a loan from somewhere else – to pay the boat loan. And Lyla and Rosaleen were not happy about it."

"It's something we can look at again. But I'm not sure there is much else to see there."

"You might be right," I said. "But we should remember that Lyla mentioned she had little to do with the business financials until recently."

"I'll have another look at it," Ethan said.

Before we left the hotel, I took some brochures from a stand near the door. "Trying to get out and about a little more," I said to Ethan as I popped them into my bag.

The porter, dressed in his red-cuffed black jacket, opened the door with his white gloved hand. "Is that your cat?" he asked as we walked through. "I've seen you walking with him before."

"Jasper ..." I said. "Yes, he's mine. You know what cats are like," I joked. "They always want to be at your side."

"Well, my sister had a cat that was the complete opposite. I think I've still got the scars to prove it." He laughed.

"They can be little rascals sometimes. But Jasper ... he's a good boy – devoted."

"I can see that," he said. "He hasn't moved from there since you arrived."

"I hope he hasn't been a bother," I said.

"Not at all," he replied. "Those eyes are something ... I don't think I've ever seen that shade of yellow before." Jasper looked straight at him. "Well, have a good afternoon, Ms Banks."

I looked at him, confused. "Do you know every visitor's name?" I asked.

"No," he laughed. "My memory is not that good. I remember you from your photo. We had heard you moved to Folly Gate ... and we've seen you around ..."

"My photo?"

"On the back of your books. My wife is a big fan. She was so excited when she heard you were in town. I think *In a Manor of Steeping* is on her bedside table at the moment."

"Oh, I see. Well, I hope she enjoys it, and tell her I said hello."

"I will," he said. "She'll be delighted. Well, I won't hold you up any longer. Enjoy the rest of your day."

"Thank you, and you too," I replied with a smile.

Jasper followed behind us as we made our way down the stairs and towards Ethan's car.

"Fans in Folly Gate ..." Ethan teased. "You might need security soon."

"I think we're all safe in that department," I said. "*In a Manor of Steeping* is not one of my best novels. In fact, it had my worst reviews."

"Well, you have a thing about your titles ..."

"It wasn't the title the critics had a problem with ... and I would rather everyone forgot about that book. But it seems like Jenifer is promoting it at her bookshop, and everyone is getting their hands on it. I might have to pay her a visit and thank her ... *personally*."

"You don't sound very happy about it."

"Oh, it's nothing. But Jenifer has never been my biggest fan – not of me, my books, or my aunt. It seems strange she would promote anything about me."

"Maybe she is trying to make amends."

"Jenifer?"

"You're right," he said with a chuckle. "Amends and Jenifer? That does seem out of character."

I left Ethan at the constabulary and drove home. With three extra witches in the house, I had expected a bit more noise when I arrived. But they all seemed to have their own interests to keep them busy. Jasper's only interest was the mackerel I had promised him at the constabulary, to stop him from disappearing down the alley again.

It surprised me how much I didn't mind having my houseguests around.

Scarlet's interest lay mostly in the library. Aunt Olivia apparently didn't leave it open. But I couldn't see any harm in leaving it open for her to explore. After all, they all knew about the Prime Spell Book, anyway. And they may come across something that helps. Aunt Olivia obviously trusted them, so I took that approach.

Amber spends a lot of time in her room, and it seems she is quite happy in there doing whatever she does.

Em, on the other hand ... you can't keep her still. If there is a clang or a bang, you can be pretty much assured it is Em.

All three of them had received pages from Aunt Olivia. But after adding them to the book, it gave no more spells or clues about what we were to do with it. We checked diligently, but there were no changes of any significance. A few pages were filling with words, but it was still all gibberish. The same gibberish we had been finding in most things to do with Aunt Olivia. They had agreed to stay and watch the house until we could figure out what was going on with the follies. Ailsa and Edlynn had kept themselves away somewhat. Shadow witches seemed to have a way of doing that to assigned witches. A natural repulsion, but it seemed to be softening. And with four of us in the house ... maybe it would help keep any other rogue witches away.

With Edlynn taking care of the shop for the rest of the day, I decided a hot shower and some afternoon tea were in order. Somehow, the house felt warm ... inviting. I left my friends to carry on with whatever they were busy with and headed upstairs, took a warm shower, changed clothes, and tried out the new glamour spell Edlynn had taught me before Kate's party. I still wasn't prepared to give up a hot bath or shower for magic – but having to style my hair, I was happy to use a wand for that. After pottering around my room, I gazed across the moors for a moment before I laid down and put my feet up on the bed. Jasper jumped up and stretched out across the bottom of the bed.

"I think I might have a little catnap," I said through a yawn.

"That sounds like the best idea you've had in days," he said. "And as I'm sure you're aware ... *catnaps* are what I do best."

CHAPTER EIGHTEEN

I ARRIVED AT THE shop as Edlynn was closing. "Ah, there you are," she said as she removed the key from the shop door. "How did you get on with Ethan?"

"Good. It didn't take long. But I went home and ended up taking a nap. I'm sorry. I wanted to get back here earlier."

"It's no problem. You must have needed it. I told you I had everything under control. I guess you are having *quite* the time at your house at the moment. Quite the houseful too – with all those shadow witches coming out of the woodwork. Be careful you don't agree to having too much on your plate, especially when you're working with Ethan as well. People will take you for everything they can, sometimes."

"I wouldn't think you would talk about Ethan like that," I said.

"I'm not talking about Ethan ... I'm talking about *the others*."

"Well, fortunately, they haven't been a bother at all. They keep themselves busy."

"I'm sure ..." Edlynn said. "Well, if you're not busy now, do you fancy an after-work glass of rosé ... at The Cidered Apple? We can catch up."

"Sure, why not?" I replied.

"But first ..." She reached into her basket before we set off down the High Street. "You're looking pale, Daisy. You can eat this on the way."

I remembered I hadn't eaten lunch or the afternoon tea I had planned on and took a large bite of the chocolate brownie.

"You have to look after yourself, Daisy. It's no wonder you're taking naps on a Monday afternoon. But I have to admit ... sometimes there's nothing better than an afternoon nap." She patted the back of my shoulder affectionately.

We continued on to The Cidered Apple. "Why do you think Aunt Olivia gave pages of the Prime Spell Book to Scarlet and Amber and Em? It doesn't seem to help us with anything. The only new spell we have retrieved has been the *Locks and Laces* spell."

"Maybe you're over-thinking it. *Maybe* you have only been shown the spell you need right now. There may be something coming. Something that you're not expecting. Olivia always had a knack for being prepared. Maybe she is helping you somehow – from the depths of the shadows."

"Maybe."

"Have you heard any more from Gwendolyn?"

"No, which makes the situation even more volatile. She is a hard woman to read. But I expect that is exactly how she wants to appear."

"I think so. I am sure she is keeping a close eye on things, though. And if I were you, I would be keeping a close eye on your new friends too. When it comes to matters involving shadow witches ... there is so much they keep secret."

"Why do you think there has always been this divide between shadows and other assigned witches?"

"Oh, I never noticed."

"You know you're lying," I said.

"I know." She linked her arm through mine. "There was a time when everything used to run smoothly down here in Devon. We all got along, used the follies, traded. But then something happened. The Cornish and

Somerset witches divided. The Southern High Coven has never been able to bring them back together again. I mean, you saw what happened in the shop. They are still at war with each other, and we are stuck in the middle. I think your aunt was trying to repair things. She worked with shadows on both sides of the county ... and they seemed to be amicable with Olivia, but still, between them, there was a rift. I have tried to keep them out of the shop at the same time, but sometimes it is inevitable ... as you saw."

"And that's all you know about it?"

"I've tried to keep out of it, to be honest. A witch knows what she needs to know when she needs to know it."

"I see. Do you think Aunt Olivia sent pages anywhere else?"

"I am almost sure of it. But to where ... is anyone's guess."

"So, you still haven't answered me. What's the problem assigned and lined witches have with shadows?"

Edlynn looked at me over her glasses and drew in a breath. "Maybe it's time you know."

The car park of The Cidered Apple filled as the town began to wind down for another day. I held the door open for Edlynn. "We'll figure this out. I promise. We all came together to secure the house, and I'm sure we can find other ways to come together in the future," I said.

"We thought so too, Daisy. But it has never eventuated."

How did I not know this? Shadows are *unassignable*? Scarlet knew it the minute she saw me, when she had collected her custom order. And now I know why they are all being so secretive. Aunt Olivia didn't give those pages away after all. And here I was, thinking they would turn up when the time was right. The Cornish witches must be refusing to say where they are – not shadow witches, nor earth witches, nor air, fire or water assigned witches were saying where the pages might be hidden. But I already knew that wouldn't stop me. If they were looking for the Prime Spell Book … then that is what they would get. And sooner than they thought.

"But Edlynn …" I asked. "How did you know—"

But before I could step through the door, a voice came from behind me, "Daisy."

"Ethan," I said.

"I was on my way to your house and saw you walking across the car park."

"Is everything okay?"

Edlynn waited in the doorway.

"I could use your help. I have to go to Kate's and—"

Edlynn stepped forward. "You better go, Daisy. It sounds important. We can catch up later. Ailsa should be here soon, anyway."

"Okay. If you're sure."

Edlynn smiled before turning and making her way to their usual booth.

"You look like you got some sleep," Ethan said as I got into the car.

I looked across at him. "You look like you've been up for days," I replied with a smile.

"Well, thanks. Not days, but it's true I haven't had a good night's sleep in a while." He reached into a paper bag before pulling out onto the road.

"Roast beef and hand-rolled butter," he said. "Baxter said you like to order it for lunch. I didn't think you'd mind eating on the job."

"Thanks," I said. "Baxter's sandwiches are pretty good, I have to admit. My dad used to buy me a roast beef and butter baguette from a little cafe around the corner from our house. They were far too big for me, but …" I cut myself off and unwrapped the small baguette. "So why are we going to Kate's house?" I asked.

"It's nothing more than standard procedure. She was the host of the party, so I want to make sure we have covered everything."

"I wouldn't think she would be up to anything untoward."

"Neither would I. But that's what we have to remember. We can't let our friendships impede an investigation. We have a woman who suddenly has a lot of money, unbeknown to anyone. And that's fine. No one has to tell everyone everything about their personal finances. But I want to make sure that there is nothing out of the ordinary going on. I am hoping to find out that she has received an inheritance or something similar. Kate hasn't ever come across as someone who is persuaded by money, but from what I heard, her party seemed a little over the top for her taste."

"I have to agree with that. But I'm not sure we are going to find much here. Her friend at the party told me she had convinced her to enjoy her money a little. Maybe she simply needed to let her hair down. A wildlife hospital is not a 9 to 5 job."

"If that is the case, then that is what we will report," Ethan said.

We arrived at Kate's house after a short drive down her potholed dirt drive, which was more of a track than a driveway. However, her thatched cottage sat neatly in a grove, immaculately gardened and painted fresh, with a flower-lined path to the front door. Kate noticed us arriving through a window and rushed out the front door to greet us.

"What's wrong here?" Ethan said as he quickly undid his seatbelt and opened the door.

I threw my sandwich on the dash and opened my door as quickly as I could. Kate had been crying and seemed to be in a state of shock.

"What is it, Kate?" Ethan said as she grabbed him and held onto him.

"It's Ellie ... well, Ben ... she just called. Ben ..." She sniffled. "Ben ... Well, Ben ... he's dead. Ellie's on her way here now."

Ethan looked across at me and took Kate by the arm. "Come inside, Kate. We'll wait for Ellie together."

I followed them both in through the cosy hallway, lined with wicker baskets filled with pet supplies for her wildlife hospital. A half-eaten hot shepherd's pie sat on her coffee table.

"Why don't I put the kettle on?" I offered.

Ethan gently nodded his head at me as he helped Kate to her chair.

I found my way to Kate's homey kitchen. There were biscuit tins and old vintage bottles lining the shelves; a large oak dining table with mismatched chairs painted in pastels and finished with gold gilding wax stood in the middle.

My wand snapped from my sleeve. I tried to put it back into my sleeve as I heard Kate's voice from the sitting room, "Can you find everything in there?"

"No problem. I've got it," I replied as I tried to fight with my stubborn wand. I relented and let it take over. The kettle turned on and two cupboards opened. One contained all her coffee, tea and teacups, and the other her teapots. "I don't suppose you know where the trays are ..." I whispered. A tall slim cupboard opened, filled with baking trays, pizza trays and muffin tins standing on their sides. And hidden in there was a beautiful silver tray. "That should do it, thank you."

My wand slipped back into my sleeve as I set the tray. Kate had lined the walls of the kitchen with photographs of family and friends, but one photograph took my eye. It was Kate and Ellie. They were younger and stood alongside Ben and Amie. Ben had his arm around Amie's waist, and it was your usual 'smiling friends on holiday' photograph. But I couldn't help noticing the look on Ellie's face. She was looking *straight* at Ben ... and it was not a look you could easily dismiss. *Love* ... is difficult to disguise. I finished organising the tray and took the tea through to the sitting room. Ethan sat next to Kate, consoling her.

"Ellie is on her way in a taxi," Ethan said. "She won't be long."

I set the tray down and poured the tea.

"I'm going to call the hospital," Ethan said.

"I'll stay with Kate." I took Ethan's place next to her on the sofa and placed a comforting hand on her knee. "It's going to be all right," I said. "Did Ellie say anything else to you?"

"Just that they did everything they could. She was so obviously in shock and already in a taxi on her way here. The hospital had told her there was nothing more she could do, and she should go and get some rest."

"Well, she won't be long. We're not far from the hospital here."

A small wooden box sat opened on the table. It was filled with four rows of five bottles and each bottle had eye dropper lids. I had seen bottles like that before. A flash of Ben and Ellie's room at the Folly View Hotel popped into my head. They looked very similar to the bottle Ben drank from when he came out of the bathroom.

"They're interesting bottles," I said. "A beautiful box. Essential oils?"

"No. They're flower essences. Amie gave them to me for my birthday."

"Have you used any of them?" I asked.

"No. I only opened them to have a look. They're not something I would use." She dabbed her nose with a tissue. "Apparently, she has been selling them at the markets or something like that. Quite a process to make them, she said."

"Oh, I might have to ask her about them," I said casually. "Maybe we could stock them in the shop."

"You're welcome to take them – try them out. Honestly, I won't use them."

"Well, in that case. If you don't mind … I'll bring them back."

"Go ahead ..." Kate sipped on her tea and looked out the window.

Ethan came back from his phone call and took a long breath. "I'm sorry, Kate. It's true. Just like the captain ... hemlock poisoning."

Kate kept her eyes on the window until her distraught sister's taxi arrived. We listened as Ellie told us that Ben had collapsed in their suite. Kate and Ellie huddled together on the sofa, and after doing everything we could to comfort the sisters, we decided it best to offer them their privacy.

"If there's anything I can do ..." I said.

Ethan handed Kate his card. "You can get me on this number – at any hour."

We let ourselves out and pulled out of the long drive, both taking a minute to compose ourselves, and drove back to town.

"What's with the box?" Ethan asked.

"It may be a hunch, but like you say, we have to look at everything. These were gifted to Kate – by Amie." I opened the box to show him the bottles. "Kate said I could take them."

"Re-gifting? I've heard people do that."

"No, I told her I would bring them back. I just wanted to look at them and see if we could sell them in the shop. However, I do have an ulterior motive."

"Why does that not surprise me?"

"If we have a serial poisoner on our hands ... these bottles look very similar to the bottles Ben drank from, when we were at the penthouse suite."

"They do?"

"Yes. And they seem to pop up a little too often for my liking. I thought I would take them to Ailsa and see if she could shed any light on them."

"Well, they really should be taken into evidence if you think something connects them with the case." He looked across at me. "Why don't you give me the bottles? I'll get them sent for analysis. You could bring them to me in about ..." – he looked at his watch – "two hours? Everything by the book, Daisy ..."

"Two hours ..."

He looked across at me again but didn't say another word.

"I can meet you then," I said. "Thank you. It *is* just a hunch at the moment."

"That's the thing about being a detective, Daisy. Most of the leads you follow on a case start with a hunch."

"Well, that doesn't sound very *logical* to me," I said. "I thought you were the kind of detective that does everything by processes and deductions and evaluations ... not *hunches*."

"Well, then it appears we are getting to know each other better ..." he said.

I smiled. "It appears, Ethan, we are."

CHAPTER NINETEEN

I HANDED KATE'S BOX to Ailsa. She stood proud amidst everything she had built in her potion room. The shelves and tables were covered in the sounds of multicoloured liquids bubbling and boiling, which changed colours as they rose up towards the ceiling. The air was damp but fragrant, and a welcome relaxation came over me whenever I entered that room. Ailsa always seemed to move so much slower in there – like everything was in order in that one little space. Jasper followed me in, raising his nose to greet the sweet aromas emanating from the bottles and jars.

"The box is not much to look at," Ailsa said. "Your standard imported rosewood box. But I like it. Simple is often best. What is it you want me to look for?"

Jasper rubbed his face across my leg as he passed. "I've seen too many of these bottles around this case," I said. "I'm giving them to Ethan so he can take them for official analysis. But I wondered if you could shed any light on what they are, and if they look like they should."

"I *have* heard about flower essences and their uses – but is there something you think I should look for in particular?"

"There is actually ... *hemlock*," I said.

"Hemlock? Well, it seems like we were right about the autumn quail."

"It looks like it."

"I am so sorry to hear about Ben," Ailsa said. "I hope you will pass on my condolences if you see Kate or Ellie before I do."

"Of course." I peered into the box. "I saw these bottles, or a bottle similar to these, when I went with Ethan to Ellie and Ben's suite—"

I was interrupted by Edlynn's voice drifting into the potion room after a gentle tap on the door.

"It's not like you to knock, Edlynn," Ailsa said.

"I'm trying something new," she said. "Don't make a big deal of it. Are these the bottles?"

"Yes," Ailsa said as she lifted one to inspect it.

"I have something that might help," Edlynn said. "I brought my notepad with my *snap images*. The image I took of Amie's bag—"

"You took an image of her bag?" I asked.

"I know not everyone approves of *snap image* spells ... I actually didn't mean to, but something must have caught my eye. It had nothing of consequence in it ... as so many of my images are not important. And I would have thought nothing more about it ... until Ailsa told me you were coming to see her about the bottles ..."

"Well, if you have something that could help ..." I said. "It would be wrong not to use it ... wouldn't it?"

"That's exactly what I thought," Edlynn replied as she quickly opened her basket.

Ailsa stayed quiet.

"What is it, then?" I asked.

"Well ..." Edlynn began, "there was your usual lipstick, perfume, cosmetics ... that sort of thing. And there were also old stubs of tickets from festivals ... and even a theatre ticket. But the one that caught my eye was for Landeel Gardens."

"I expect if she is making flower essences then garden visits would be on her agenda," Ailsa said. "But Landeel Gardens? Are you sure?"

"Yes, I'm sure," Edlynn said. "And this was a season ticket ..."

"And?" I asked.

"As it happens," Edlynn continued, "we know a lot about this garden – most witches do."

"Why is that?" I asked.

"Well," Ailsa continued for Edlynn, "*Landeel Gardens* happen to possess the largest poison garden in England. We better get a move on."

I watched as Ailsa took a few drops from each bottle and, using an antique she had bought from the Folly Gate Fair, tested for the ingredients hidden in the bottles. "It shouldn't take long," she said. "I don't even think the trader really knew what he was selling when I bought this contraption. Alchemists would do things we probably shouldn't mention for one of these." She tapped the side of the contraption with her index finger. "I'll make us a tea and it should be ready."

After following Ailsa through to her kitchen and making tea, we made our way back into the potion room, tea in hand, with Jasper at my heels.

Ailsa picked up the long brass tray fitted with smaller trays on one edge, where she had previously extracted and added a drop from each of Kate's bottles. "Let me look at the colour chart," she said. "We don't want to see anything olive green, apparently." She gently removed the lithium type paper from the top of the contraption with a pair of small silver tweezers. "Well, there you have it," she said.

And Edlynn gasped, as my eyes widened.

I stepped back from the locked constabulary doors. Maybe Ethan had stopped by The Cidered Apple for a Hunter's Chicken. A sign with an emergency contact number hung in the window, but he wasn't expecting me for another hour. I turned and walked back to my van.

"We'll leave it here," I said to Jasper. "He'll call when he sees the van. There's someone I want to talk to, and it's only a short walk."

Jasper jumped across from the passenger seat as I placed the box in the back of the van, and we made our way towards the Folly View Hotel.

"Shouldn't you be going with Ethan?" Jasper asked as we headed up the hotel's steps.

"Oh," I said. "This isn't police business. This is about *Liv's Lumières.*"

"Uhuh ..." Jasper said, tinged with a little disbelief.

"It will only take a minute. Wait here."

The porter held the door open for me. "Welcome back to the Folly View, Ms Banks."

"Thank you," I said.

"Back on official business?" he asked. "Sorry, I shouldn't have asked that." He nodded his head politely and apologised again.

"It's okay. *Unofficial* business," I said.

"Well, enjoy your time with us," he replied.

I walked across the lobby, as I had done with Ethan, but this time I was looking for Amie. I thought I would look around the hotel first and see if I could find her before I asked reception. It could be a little more difficult to visit without Ethan. And, if you believe in luck, it was on my side tonight. I looked across the bar and saw Amie sitting at a balcony window with an evening cocktail in her hand. I walked straight over to her.

"Amie ..."

"Oh, Daisy." She jumped a little. "You caught me off guard."

"Sorry, I didn't mean to startle you," I said.

"That's okay. I had my head in the clouds. After hearing about Ben, I thought I would come down and have something to *soothe my nerves*, as they say."

"I understand. And I'm very sorry to hear about your friend."

Amie drew in a long breath. "It's quite the view from here during the day," she said. "But now ... I can't see anything in the darkness of it all. It's probably one of Ben's last views."

I pressed my lips together.

She continued, "I'm still here for a few days. I had planned to spend them with Kate and Ellie. But with everything that's happened ... I spoke with Ellie earlier and offered to help ... or meet her at Kate's, but she insisted I get some rest. Ben's family would arrive soon and ... well, you know ... I'm not family. I even offered to help with the wildlife hospital. But they insisted they would be fine taking care of it. They're like that ... independent."

"Well, maybe it's for the best. It's quite a shock and there's not a lot more you can do. Sometimes being there from a distance offers more support than we know. There *is* something else I wanted to talk to you about, though. I hope you don't mind, but I wanted to catch you before you left Folly Gate."

"You did?"

"Yes, about your flower essences."

"Oh, what about them?"

"I wondered if you might be interested in supplying some for *Liv's Lumières*. I saw them at Kate's and thought they would be a perfect addition to our shop."

She sipped on her cocktail. "Oh, I'm sorry, Daisy. Those bottles were the last of them. I was getting rid of the last of my stock before I leave Folly Gate and head back to India."

"India?"

135

"Yes. I have lived in Pushkar on and off over the years. I wanted to make an announcement at the party to let them know I was going back, but Kate and Ellie were having such a job trying to get Ben home, I never had a chance to say anything." Her eyes dropped. "And the saddest thing about it all is that Saturday night was supposed to be our last … *hurrah*."

After declining Amie's dinner invitation, I knew I had to get back to Ethan quickly. He needed to question her before she left Folly Gate. The hotel was a short walk from the constabulary, but I could make it even quicker cutting through the alleyways. Jasper sat waiting at the bottom of the stairs.

"Come on," I said. "Let's take a shortcut back to Ethan."

The alleyways and shortcuts hidden throughout Folly Gate would take some time to figure out, but I had Jasper. And there is nothing, or *no one*, better to help you find your way around than a local – shall we say – *alley cat*. I followed Jasper as he darted this way and that, past cafes and shops that I hadn't visited yet. We passed a dimly lit milliner with a vivid red and gold badged door. I made a mental note to stop by one day. As we turned into a quiet, dark and empty alleyway, I flicked my wand to give us some light.

"Lost something, have we?" a voice came from deep within the alleyway.

"Hello?" I spoke out into the darkness as I snapped my wand back into my sleeve.

"It's Morton," he said as he stepped into a sliver of moonlight.

"Oh," I said. "What are you doing creeping around alleyways in the dark of the night?"

"I could ask you the same thing," he replied.

"I'm helping DC Fairfield. We're on our way to see him now."

"I see," he said. "Well, I'd be a little more careful about using your wand in the alleyways ... anyone could see you."

"Thanks for the warning," I said, a little dismissively.

Morton stepped closer. "How is your folly problem going? Have you visited the man in the small house yet?"

"Not yet. I've had some other matters that needed attention."

"Well, I wouldn't leave it too long. The thing about follies is, unfortunately, alchemists cannot be of much help. Since we lost the hermitages, anyone can creep in and out of them ... if they know how to, of course."

"What do you mean the *hermitages*?"

Morton looked pleased. "Well, I'm glad you asked. There is one quite near here – sealed off now, though – stacked with Quaker headstones. It seems you don't know about the agreements we used to share."

"There was an agreement? Between witches and alchemists?"

"Yes," Morton replied. "Centuries ago, the alchemists would watch over suspected folly entrances and report who entered and left them. Mostly only to our Order, but if needed, we would share that information ... for a price, of course."

"And what happened?"

"After a time, it became rumoured throughout society that there were magical folly systems hidden behind the hermitages. We knew the truth, as did the witches. But nobody ever confirmed it to be true, of course. Why would we? Why would you? But the wealthiest of landowners began building follies in their gardens and keeping hermits to watch over them, even asking them to grow beards to look more druid-like. Maybe they thought it might sway the folly travellers into trading their secrets. Nobody knows the real motive. But we knew the hermitages were being watched over by alchemists who were usually under some sort of disciplinary action. They were paying the price for their *misdeeds*. But the landowners kept building them with no assurances that a folly built by them would open any kind of magical system. They built their hermits small homes and had them live in their hermitages, delighting their guests with their *living garden ornament*. The landowners would provide the hermit with food and shelter, and they would make a deal of sorts. There was a time when the Order of Alchemists became quite involved, offering their own alchemists to these wealthy landowners in the hope they might discover how to move through the follies as freely as the witches could. However, the alchemists they supplied were usually carrying reputations of little regard, and they found *nothing* ... apparently. Eventually, the wealthy landowners gave up keeping hermits as garden decorations – society frowned upon it. And by the late 1700s, the gardens of the wealthy became modern landscapes, adopting the German and Scandinavian gnomes as the fashionable way to decorate them. But, alas ... over time, the follies became of less importance to the alchemists – well, officially, anyway."

I looked down at Jasper.

"However," Morton continued. "It looks like you have more important matters to take care of than an unsolicited history lesson. I won't keep you any longer. And when you're ready, *remember* ... your map is waiting for you." He turned to continue on his way.

"Morton ... wait," I said and drew in a breath. "I have a problem ... and I could use your help."

CHAPTER TWENTY

AFTER DISCUSSING MY PROBLEM with Morton, we headed straight to Ethan. The dull blue light of the constabulary shone across the car park.

"I don't think this is such a good idea, Daisy," Jasper said.

"What? Speaking with Morton or convincing Ethan that Amie may have something to do with all of this."

"Maybe both."

"Well, we have the night to consider it."

"It might be convenient to make a deal with Morton, Daisy, but I don't know that Gwendolyn will approve."

"It's a risk we have to take. If we can get to the man in the small house, he might be able to tell us about anyone using or asking for a crossover potion. And with Morton's tools we will be able to see what we can draw out here, in Folly Gate. Don't you think that maybe if we could become allies with the alchemists, we could put the Southern Covens far ahead of anyone else, further ahead than anyone has been for centuries?"

"You might convince Edlynn and Ailsa ... even Scarlet and her friends ... but Gwendolyn, I'm not sure you have much of a chance. The Cornish and Somerset witches can't even come together."

"Well, at least we know why now. Witches and their secrets. If we could retrieve the pages from the Cornish witches and put them together with what we have from the Somerset shadow witches, we could return the Prime Spell Book to its former glory. And we would all have access to spells that may have been missing for centuries."

"Not everyone wants unity, Daisy. I would hazard a guess that with what is going on in the follies, someone is looking for power: power over the follies, power over movement, trade ... and let's not forget ... the Folly Gate Fair."

"You might be right. I mean, the fair is a good time, that's for sure, but why would someone want power over a good time?"

"I guess you already suspect there is far more to the fair than meets the eye. The VIP area, for instance ... no one ever knows who's in there. There are a lot of caravans, but few fair-goers are ever seen coming and going from them. There are rumours of traders moving items through there ... old antiquities ... mysterious items. They don't abide by the usual rules of the fair, and no one ever questions them. Even I have tried over the years to get past the security, and there is no chance – not without a personal invitation. Even your aunt couldn't get back there. I have always suspected there was more behind the High Coven. I mean, you can't tell me you believe Gwendolyn lives in that huge old building by herself, only ever leaving it to enforce High Coven or Grand Coven business. She is full of secrets, and I have known her to be quite volatile on occasion, but no one has ever had the courage to ask her what goes on there. They passed the High Coven on to her through her line, but no one knows who she might leave it to ... But all that aside, I think an alchemist makes for a bad bedfellow, Daisy. They will wait until you come looking for them. They know you'll eventually want something from them, so they wait until they can strike the best deal ... But I don't think it's only Gwendolyn you have to worry about. The other covens may find it very difficult to forgive the alchemists ... even if they are of help."

"What do you mean?"

"The trials ... Many witches proclaim the alchemists were involved. No one has ever proven anything, of course, but they rose to places of power in society and were determined to get their hands on any information about the follies and magic. Some say the alchemists believe the follies may hide the Stone of Knowledge, and the Order makes them look like they are of no significance to anyone, on purpose. But finding an alchemist that would admit it ... that's another matter. Most people think they are simply tourist attractions, or a reason to charge people to visit gardens ... but the alchemists think they are much more. I don't know that Gwendolyn would allow any kind of alliance. We lost a lot of good witches in those trials. A dreadful ... awful time for your line, especially in Pittenweem. *May they rest in the shadows.* A torturous time. And I am not sure Gwendolyn would want to revisit or encourage any kind of enthusiasm for the alchemists. Why do you think their tools attract witches? Have you ever thought it might be by design?"

"Well, it might be. But I can't visit the man in the small house to ask him yet, anyway. I have the cake competition to enter, remember? If there are any witches sneaking around Folly Gate, I should be able to find them. And the fact that alchemists' tools attract witches *could* be of use to us."

"I don't know about that, Daisy – I'd be careful."

"Well, I appreciate the concern, Jasper. Now let's get to Ethan before Amie suspects anything and tries to leave town."

I grabbed the box from the back of the van and entered the station, with Jasper at my heels. Ethan was filing some papers in the front office and smiled when he saw us. "You two really are inseparable."

"You know what cats are like," I said, returning his smile. "We've just come from Folly View ... after talking to Amie ..." I paused for his reaction.

"You know you shouldn't have done that, Daisy. Everything has to be done *by* the book." He didn't look angry ... but he did look disappointed.

"I wasn't visiting her about the case, Ethan. I went to the hotel to ask her about a business proposition ... for *Liv's Lumières* ..."

Ethan raised an eyebrow. "And what was this business proposition ..."

"Her flower essences," I said. "I went to ask her if she would be interested in supplying us with them to stock in the shop."

"Is that so?" He smirked. "And what did she say?"

"She said that she couldn't because they were the last bottles, as she was selling up and returning to India."

"India?" Ethan didn't hide his surprise.

"She said she has spent a lot of time there, over the years."

"Well, that *is* interesting," he said.

I tapped the box before sliding it across to Ethan. "I think you should get these analysed as quickly as you can. There may be something of interest in there."

Ethan stepped towards the counter and lowered his voice, "Did Ailsa find something?"

"Yes, she did ... just as we suspected."

"You know I can't do anything about this until I have it officially confirmed. We have to have evidence before we can follow anything up with Amie."

I looked him in the eye. "I am simply dropping off an item that may be of interest to you. That is all."

Ethan looked around as if to make sure no one was listening. "Well, thank you, Daisy. I'll look into it first thing in the morning."

I leant in and lowered my voice, "You can't do anything sooner? She could leave."

"No, I'm sorry. We can't arrest someone on a *hunch*. But I'll let you know as soon as I know anything."

I kept my voice low and slipped him a piece of paper. "*Landeel Gardens*. I think you'll find she's been growing and brewing more than just flowers."

"I'll check it out," he said cautiously, making sure we were still alone. "And I have something interesting to tell you, too."

"You do?"

"Did you know Kate hired a photographer for the party?"

"Yes. I saw him taking photos all night. I was hoping I might get some copies, before all this happened – not the memories anyone needs hanging on their wall now, though."

"I agree. But he wasn't only taking photos, Daisy. He filmed the entire night, too. He set his cameras up in the dining room and out on the deck."

I leant in closer. "I never noticed them."

"I think he meant it to be that way. People aren't always themselves when they know they're being filmed."

"Did you find anything?"

"I don't know yet. He said he would email the raw footage through to me. There's not much more we can do right now."

"Well, then ... I suppose I'll leave it with you."

"Yep. Go and put your feet up," he said, as he lifted the rosewood box from the counter.

"Thanks, Ethan. I might just do that." I scooped up Jasper and turned to leave before whispering into his little ear, "Let's get out of here, Jasper. We have some business to take care of at home."

The three witches stood in my aunt's library, backed up against the fire's hearth. I flicked my wand and slammed the door shut. Jasper stood tall beside me, his gentle purrs transformed into a low growl.

"Admit it!" I bellowed at them. "My aunt never gave you those pages! You stole them!"

Scarlet held her hands out in front of her. "No, Daisy. You have it all wrong. Please ... you have to believe us."

Amber and Em pleaded alongside her.

"Why should I believe you?"

"Your aunt gave us the pages from the Prime Spell Book because someone ... somehow ... had stolen pages," Scarlet continued.

"So, you thought you would come here and get your hands on the rest? The Banks witches have protected the Prime Spell Book for centuries and I intend to keep it that way. How many more pages do you have hidden?"

"*None* ... none, Daisy," Scarlet replied.

"Well, now I know why you're so interested in Aunt Olivia's library. No doubt you've been searching through every book."

"Daisy ..." Scarlet stepped towards me. "That's not true. Well, not in the way you think, anyway." She dropped her hands. "The truth is I know this library better than anyone here."

"What do you mean?"

Her voice softened, "It's why I hid her wand ... in here. Right behind this book." Scarlet stepped over and removed *A Great Folly Gate History* from the shelf. "You found it behind here, didn't you?"

Jasper shifted his large paw forwards. "How did you know that? How long have you been sneaking around here? What else have you three been up to? I want you out of my house!"

"No, Daisy ... please ... just listen. You don't understand."

"You had better make it quick," I said and kept my wand pointed firmly in her direction.

She replaced the book on its shelf and looked across at Amber and Em before looking back at me. "I ... I found her, Daisy. It was me ..."

"Who?" I questioned her.

A single tear rolled down Scarlet's cheek. "Olivia ... *lifeless* ... slumped over against the Rowan tree on Heathbury Cliff."

Amber's hand shot up to cover her mouth. Em strolled over and took a seat in my aunt's reading chair. Her mouse scuttled across the floor after her and ran up her leg, before finding his way to her blazer pocket. His two little back paws kicked out of the top of her pocket as he pulled himself in and tucked his little tail inside. She pulled out a bag of sugared almonds and shoved one in her mouth, her eyes wide as she dropped one into the top pocket for her *familiar*.

"Aunt Olivia ..." My arm dropped as my wand snapped back into my sleeve, and Jasper returned to his usual feline self. The library door gently clicked and swung open.

Scarlet reached her arms out towards me. "I didn't know what to do. She was gone, Daisy. I took her wand and hid it in here. She had always spoken of her hope for you returning to Folly Gate one day. It was the safest place I could think to hide it."

I sat down on the floor and rested my back against the bookshelves. "Why didn't you tell me?"

"We were trying to protect you. But we don't know against what or who yet."

"Who? You think someone did this to her?"

"I called the police – *straightaway*. It surprised me when your police officer friend didn't recognise me the night he stopped by to check on you. But with my face covered in a mud mask ..." she continued her story. "They said it was a heart attack and we haven't yet been able to come to any other conclusion. But your aunt was a strong, healthy woman. And for her to go walking along the cliffs without Jasper ... well, something doesn't feel right. She had been so vague about giving us the pages and we didn't question it. *A witch's business is her own.*"

"How do you know someone has stolen the other pages?"

"It's the only conclusion that makes any sense. She was protecting the Prime Spell Book – as the Banks witches have always done."

Jasper purred a sad and hollow sound. My eyes welled up as I held my head in my hands. "How am I supposed to trust anything you say?"

Scarlet rushed over and took a place on the floor next to me. "We're going to figure this out, Daisy," she said as she put her arm around me and cradled my face with her hand. "If it was a heart attack, we will accept that ... but if it was something else ... something that might still be a threat—"

"Well, I don't know about you ..." Em interrupted, as she casually popped another almond into her mouth, "I think something scared her."

"Something scared her? Like what?" I asked.

"I don't know," she replied through her almonds. "But whatever happened ... I think it was something or someone that scared her *deep* into the *shadows.*"

Chapter Twenty-One

Edlynn poured me an Earl Grey tea. "Let's sit out the back. The shop is quiet this morning. Oh, and take these." She passed me a delicate porcelain plate of biscuits. "Ailsa baked them fresh this morning: lavender shortbread." Edlynn sat down and pulled in her chair to the table.

I made myself comfortable before reaching into my bag and placing the bottle Morton had given me on the table.

Edlynn peered down at it, being careful to keep her hands away. "Well, I have to say, it all sounds a little absurd to me, Daisy. We're to take it to a *man in a small house*? And what do you think is in the bottle?"

"Morton called it *Raphael's pigment*. Apparently, master artists like Raphael used it in their paintings. And, as the man in the small house is the Artist for the Order, Morton said it could persuade him to help us with a crossover potion."

"Well, if you think it's going to help, we have nothing to lose, I suppose. But how do we *know* it will help?"

"We don't," I said. "But it's the only lead I have to go on at the moment."

"Have you spoken with Gwendolyn about this?" Edlynn asked. "I'm not sure she'd agree."

"No. First I have to find the proof it is not one of our shadow witches that is causing the destruction in the follies. I can't understand why someone would want to destroy them, anyway. As it is now, we only use them for travel."

"I know that's how it might seem to you, Daisy. But I think the bigger problem is regarding *what* someone could move through them ... and *who* could move through them. Someone with access to a crossover potion could cause all the trouble they wanted and then be on the other side of the country within a few minutes."

"My map doesn't even stretch that far yet."

"Well, alchemists are renowned for their cartography. I don't believe Morton and his family have remained printers for so long without reason. I am sure there are a lot of maps that have passed through his hands over the years."

"Including the one he has offered me." I reached into my bag again. "And this one – to find the man in the small house."

"Let me see it," Edlynn said.

Jasper jumped up from the ground onto the chair next to me, before settling himself on the table and keeping a keen eye on Edlynn as she unfolded the map.

"Oh, I know exactly where this is," Edlynn said as she laid it out flat. "But I don't remember anything about a *small house* ..."

"Morton said I was to use this when I got there." I passed her the small river stone, with its perfect circular hole in the middle.

"A fae stone ..."

"I've never used one before," I said.

"Well, they can only be used during the four hinges of the day: sunrise, midday, sunset and midnight. When were you thinking of visiting him?"

"I haven't decided. The Cake Off is today and I need to get the cakes to them before 11am."

"That only leaves you an hour?" Edlynn looked at me curiously. "I didn't see you bring in any cakes."

I sipped on my tea. "I might need your help with that."

"Early lunch?" Edlynn smiled cheekily and scurried inside to turn the shop sign around. She turned back to see me waiting for her. "I can help with the ingredients ... and you can add your shadow items. How many cakes do we need?"

"Just the one cake," I replied. "But I want sixty cupcakes ... frosted ... and with a single sweet cherry on top."

"You've lost me," Edlynn said. "I thought we were entering the Cake Off."

"We are. But we are also giving away samples – with a 20% discount voucher for *Liv's Lumières*."

She looked surprised. "That's very generous ..."

"That is how I want it to look," I said as I reached into my pocket and pulled out a small brass compass. "Morton gave me this, too."

"An alchemist's tool. What are you doing carrying this around? Put it away, Daisy. You'll only attract the wrong kind of witch. Alchemists are notorious for their attraction tools."

Jasper stood next to me, listening intently, maybe hoping Edlynn would convince me otherwise. "I know, Edlynn," I said. "And that's exactly why I asked him for the tool."

"Morton is really going out of his way to help you, Daisy. Are you not concerned with how much it will cost you?"

"I know it will cost me. But I have thought it over ... *with Jasper* ... and I believe the cost is worth the risk."

"I gather Gwendolyn doesn't know about this either."

"No. We all know what most witches think about alchemists. But Morton has been helpful, especially with trying to find out who could be using a crossover potion. And I will do whatever it takes to save the reputation of our coven and the shadows attached to it."

"We have attached shadows now?"

"Scarlet, Amber and Em all offered the pages that Aunt Olivia gave them. And they have been honest about being closer to Aunt Olivia's death than we were led to believe."

"What do you mean?" Edlynn asked.

"Last night, Scarlet told me she was the person who found Aunt Olivia. She went straight to the police and there didn't seem to be anything untoward about the story."

Edlynn's voice rose, "We were never told. Why didn't she tell us? We were told a dog walker found her."

"I expect they were protecting her anonymity. And, as you well know, shadows tend to keep their business to themselves ... as any witch is entitled to do. There *are* advantages to building the divide between shadows and other witches. And there must have been a reason Aunt Olivia wanted them to have those pages. Whatever that reason is, it's the reason I want them so close to me right now."

"I must admit, it makes sense for Olivia to give them the pages, Daisy. They would have to come together before the Prime Spell Book could work again. And if she had been so sure it was the right decision, I suppose we have to accept that and see where it leads us."

"Well, I am hoping that you and Ailsa could be the ones to forge new relationships between covens and shadows. Not everyone gets to choose their line ... in fact, no one really does. Having the Somerset shadows on our side could help not only protect the Prime Spell Book, but also protect it from the Cornish shadows."

"Why do you think we should protect it from the Cornish witches? Why shouldn't we protect it from the Somerset shadows? Maybe you have invited the enemy in."

"I don't think that's the case. And if Aunt Olivia thought that was the case, she wouldn't have given them the pages."

"How do you know they are not lying about finding Olivia?"

"I don't. I only know that Scarlet wouldn't have a reason to lie about that. She took quite a risk telling me. She didn't know how I might react, so I figure there must be an element of trust there. But I am keeping an open mind. Right now, I don't know what to do with the information, or if it makes any difference. Scarlet may have seen no need to tell us before now. All I know at the moment is that Gwendolyn suspects us, and, as the head of the coven, I have to do everything I can to make sure that I protect you and Ailsa from anything that might come from the three shadows. Maybe, for now, it's best if you don't bring it up with them, and we keep looking for the rest of the pages and whoever is messing with the follies. Gwendolyn is obliged to look at me as the prime suspect ... although I'm not sure she really thinks I would be capable of destroying the follies: I have no motive. But I do think she is hoping that I might lead her to some answers. When I found Aunt Olivia's wand, she knew I was capable of finding it, but she was simply wondering how long it would take me to locate it. I think she knows there is something I can lead her to. And that's why she put me in charge of the coven ... even though I was a brand-new witch. There must be something I know, or something I have access to that nobody else does. But, for now, I need you to help me make these shadow cakes, get them to the Cake Off, and stand back and see if we can flush out any witches that are unaccounted for in Folly Gate. If I succeed, then at least I have something to take to Gwendolyn."

"And when will we go to the man in the small house?" Edlynn asked.

"As soon as we can."

"You won't convince Ailsa to go to Somerset," Edlynn said.

"I assumed as much. I thought it would have to be you and me," – I turned to Jasper – "and Jasper, if you're interested?"

"Whenever you're ready," he replied.

"He's in," I said to Edlynn. "Now, how long will it take to make these cakes?"

"If you have the recipe ... a *flick of a wand*."

I reached into my pocket and passed her a folded recipe. "I found one of Aunt Olivia's ..."

Edlynn's eyes lit up. "Good, then we'll get the Cake Off out of the way and make our way to Somerset. We should arrive at the man in the small house around midnight, making perfect time to use the fae stone." Edlynn flicked her wand from her sleeve. "Sounds like a good plan, Daisy," she said as she raised her wand towards the kitchen. "Let's bake!"

CHAPTER TWENTY-TWO

I WALKED WITH EDLYNN towards the large sign for the Folly Gate Cake Off directing us to the bunting-covered town hall. Jasper left us at the door and found himself a spot under a tree nestled in a small green garden, lined with wooden sitting benches. I had been told that the garden had been the site of many public hangings centuries ago, and, on a still night, residents could hear the creaking of the gallows and the jeering crowd drift across the cobbled streets of Folly Gate. All that remained today was a large, forgotten flat stone, propped up in the ground, carved with an epitaph to those that had fallen there.

Edlynn promised to find us a spot close to the judge's table – somewhere with a clear view. I walked back to the car park to bring in more cupcakes from the van. When I returned, I tried to prop open the town hall door with my foot but missed, and the door shut with a bang.

"Let me get that for you, Daisy," Ethan's voice came from behind me.

"Thank you." I smiled. "Why don't you grab one off the top there? Good old-fashioned cherry cakes."

He grabbed a box and held the door open. "After you ..."

He followed me over to the table where Edlynn was struggling with setting up our display. She had a way with table settings ... well, her wand did anyway, but the Folly Gate Cake Off was not the place for a quick flick from her sleeve.

Edlynn turned and passed Ethan a cupcake. "Try this. Let me know what you think? Are we in with a chance?" She waited eagerly as Ethan bit into the cherry cupcake.

"Well," he said. "You have my vote." He took another bite and crumpled up the cupcake case. "Do you have more cakes to bring in? I could give you a hand," he offered.

"Just the competition cake," I said. "And I'll be okay with that. Edlynn, do you want to get the tags we need and we'll get our cake on the table?"

Ethan looked across at the other tables. "It's good to see you getting into the community spirit, Daisy. I just didn't think baking would be the way you went in."

"I thought it would be a bit of fun ... and I do love a trip to Home Sweet Scone."

"Well, the best of luck to you." Ethan smiled.

"You think I need it?"

"I'm sure you don't," he replied. "You baked the best cherry cake I've ever tasted. What time is the winner being announced?"

"Around 4pm I think."

"I'll make sure to pop back and watch you take your victory!" He clenched his fists in the air in a show of triumph. "You give them a run for their money!"

I laughed as I followed him out of the building to bring in the competition entry cake. He held the door open for me again. "Thank you," I said. "Have you heard any more about the captain ... or Ben?"

"Nothing new on the case yet," he said. "I might head up to Exeter and see if I can get things moving, and stop in and see Mum while I'm there. It won't be long before we have something to work with. I'll let you know."

"Okay. Well, I'll see you around 4 then."

He looked puzzled.

"For the competition ..." I said.

"Oh right, yes, the competition. Sorry, I have a lot on my mind. Folly Gate is not such a quiet place at the moment. It's like there's something in the air, Dais' ... like something is brewing ..."

A loud clap of thunder caught us off guard as we reached my van.

"Ooh, you might be right," I said with a chuckle. "Don't tell me you have another *hunch* about something?"

"Maybe I do ... but I'm not even sure what about. Anyway ... it's silly, really. Maybe it's just the storm coming in. But Folly Gate pays their detectives to keep their rational thoughts, not to be working on whims."

"Well, I'll keep an eye out for anything unusual."

"It's good to have you on my side, Daisy." He smiled as he turned to leave. "And drive safely in this storm. The winds are going to be pretty strong."

"I will," I said, slightly surprised at his demeanour.

"I'll see you at 4."

I casually waved him off before removing the cake from the back of the van. Our entry for the competition looked perfectly decorated with sweet cherry buttercream elegantly piped on the top, and almond slivers coating the sides. It was a tall cake: two cakes sliced into four layers, stacked with butter-cream and sweet cherry jam. When I returned to the hall, Edlynn was filling in the necessary paperwork for entry. We walked to the judges' table together and gently placed our shadow cake on it. No one was any the wiser. A visitor to the competition commented that it looked delicious, and we offered her a sample from our table. I watched carefully as she took a mouthful. Her lips pursed together; her eyes closed. "Oh, that tastes even better than it looks," she said, "if that's possible. I think you have a winner there. Good luck in the competition."

Before we knew it, a long line of people was queuing for a cupcake. In fact, the line for our table was the longest in the hall. One by one we watched them sample our cake and everyone said the same thing: *Delicious!*

We had seven cupcakes left by 4pm. I turned the brass compass in my hand and looked at Edlynn. "Well, it seems my plan may have all been for naught. Everyone thought the cupcakes were delicious."

"Well, it was worth a try," Edlynn said. "I did, however, think Morton's tool would have attracted at least one witch."

"Me too," – I looked at Edlynn with disappointment – "but maybe we can still leave with a ribbon."

Edlynn placed a comforting hand on my shoulder. "The judges are about to walk the table now, so it shouldn't be long."

We watched as the judges pointed and took notes about the cakes, discussing them behind blank cards and lifted clipboards. Eventually, Penelope Black rang a small bell to announce the beginning of judging. They instructed us to label our tags anonymously for the competition, but really all they had to do was look around the tables to see which cake belonged to who.

Penelope Black took up her microphone and began introducing the judges when we noticed Dawn enter the hall. She walked swiftly towards the judging table and whispered into Penelope's ear. Penelope nodded in approval to Dawn's request before continuing, "And our last judge today, filling in for Jenifer Penton, her daughter Dawn."

"Thank goodness for small mercies," I said under my breath to Edlynn.

We caught Dawn's eye, and she threw us a quick smile before being handed her standard clipboard and pen. The judges moved through four cakes before gathering around ours. Penelope continued, "And now we have an entry of an old-fashioned cherry cake."

The appointed cake slicer handed each judge a small piece. They turned their forks in their mouths, making sure they got every last bit of the cake and buttercream off their forks. They looked back and forth at each other before one judge asked for another piece, which I believe was rather unheard of in these types of competitions. But it was not the judges I had my eyes on ... *and* it was not a slice of cake that was stuck in my throat ... it was words – words that couldn't find their way out of my mouth.

Edlynn leant into me. "She doesn't seem to like it, Daisy."

Dawn looked across at the other judges, her face grimaced and her lips taut.

Penelope held the microphone up to Dawn. "It's not for you, Dawn?"

Dawn took a napkin to her mouth. "Oh, I'm so sorry. But I've never been much of a sour cherry person."

"Sour cherry?" Edlynn asked me.

I kept my voice low, "We both know that we filled our cake with sweet cherries, Edlynn ... not sour ..."

Edlynn dropped her head in disappointment, not because our chances of winning had narrowed – it wasn't that at all. Shadow cakes, as I had learned from Ailsa, will without fail be the worst thing a witch has ever tasted. And unfortunately, we had not only served our friend the worst thing she had ever tasted ... but we may have also found our rogue witch.

I parked the van at the front of my house and opened the door. It had been a silent drive home from the Cake Off; the ticking of our minds quietened both of us. I let Jasper out and grabbed the few things left to bring back home. The front door greeted us, opening slowly as if it knew to join us in the silence.

Edlynn stroked the blue ribbon in her hand. "Well, at least we won. That's something, I suppose."

"Of course. We would always win with a shadow cake," I said.

"I can't believe what we witnessed. I mean, Dawn was always with your aunt ... and there was a time we even thought of asking her to join our coven, but we had no idea ... *or* maybe Olivia did, and didn't tell us. A witch's business is her own, though, and we would never have questioned it."

"That's just it. A witch's business *is* her own. But what if the witch in question doesn't know she is a witch? Is it another witch's place to tell her?"

"I am sure there are rules around this, but I've never heard of a witch not knowing she was a witch. Maybe Gwendolyn knows something ... but if a witch didn't want someone to know they were a witch ... well, that's a different matter."

"Do you honestly think Dawn would deliberately keep that hidden from us ... from Aunt Olivia? I didn't know I was a witch until I came to Folly Gate. I think it would be perfectly reasonable for Dawn not to know."

"I know *you* didn't know, Daisy. But quite a few people did. Your father ... your aunt ... Ailsa ... and of course I knew. But it must be a chosen life, and it's not our business to decide these things."

"Well, if all of you knew about me ... even when *I* didn't, then it would make sense that someone other than us could know about Dawn, too."

"I would think you're right, Daisy. Maybe Gwendolyn would know?"

"Maybe she does. But first we have to think about how we look to Gwendolyn. Witches having no idea there was a rogue witch staring us in the face? I don't want to create more suspicion around us."

"What shall we do?" Edlynn asked.

"We'll keep with our original plan. Visit the man in the small house and see if we can come up with a solution on the way. We have to find out why Dawn has never been *assigned*. And I think I know just where to start."

Chapter Twenty-Three

I FOLLOWED JASPER AND Edlynn inside the house, closed the front door behind us and called out to my houseguests, but there was no response.

"They must be getting a head start on their ritual," Edlynn said. "We'll have an extra special one on the next full moon."

I smiled at Edlynn. "It is a shame we couldn't join them for this one. But who knows, maybe by the next moon we can all have one together."

Edlynn remained silent and pressed her lips together. "We better get a move on."

I fed Jasper, drew the front curtains and left a light on, before we packed up the van with the few things needed for our trip to Somerset. It would take a few hours to get there, and Edlynn wanted to stop in at a friend's house on the way. I agreed, as the visit would allow us a break and also meant we would be right on time to use the fae stone at midnight. Edlynn held the door of the van open for Jasper as he jumped up onto the front bench seat which could fit three people snugly. I laid down a small blanket for him and settled him in the middle of us, safe and secure for our journey.

Edlynn closed her door, pulled her seatbelt across, and continued our conversation from inside the house, "Do you really think Jenifer could hide the fact she's a witch from Dawn ... from everyone? Surely, we would have known. Like I've said before, she had a lot to do with your aunt for many years, but she stopped coming to the shop – and your aunt never said why. I hope you're not right about Jenifer, Daisy. If she had kept that secret for so long ... *and* from Dawn, there must be a reason. And it would have to be an important one."

I started the van and cracked open my window a little before reversing out of the driveway. "It's just a hunch, at the moment, but it would make sense of some of her strange antics. But Edlynn ... I hope I'm not right, too."

"Well, Jenifer is always involved in *plenty* of antics ... we all know that. In fact, she is probably Folly Gate's queen of antics!" Edlynn said grandly.

"Her antics may be a cover for something more sinister ... but don't worry, we will get to the bottom of it."

We continued our drive out of the moors as the sun set over the beaches of Torquay, until we reached the M5 motorway heading north. It was another hour's drive until we reached Edlynn's friend's house. She had taken a quick nap as I drove, and the quiet gave me time to consider all the reasons why Jenifer Penton might hide the fact she was a witch ... and more importantly, why would she hide it from her daughter? Too much was falling into place as I considered it. The constant mistaken packages she would bring to me already opened ... Once, maybe twice, might have been a mistake, but could it be that she was looking for something? The broken relationship with my aunt ... wanting me out of Folly Gate ... her absolute disdain at the sight of me. I had felt something strange about her from the minute I met her. I mean, if she despised me so much, why did she always seem so involved with my business? Wouldn't she just stay out of my way? Could there be something I had that she needed? That could be likely ... I mean, I was only just beginning to find out what my aunt had her wand dipped into.

"Left at the next junction," Edlynn said as she rose from her nap. "You're going to love Tiggy. She always has some exciting story about what she's been getting up to. I don't know how she does it. She is one of those *fly-by-night* witches. And she has a broom collection like no other. She said she has found something special for me. I didn't think you would mind stopping in to visit her. We'll stop for a comfort break and be where we need to be for midnight."

"It's perfectly fine with me," I said.

"And Jasper ... Rosie will be there." She turned in her seat to smile at him. "You remember Rosie, don't you?"

Jasper sat up and looked over the dashboard.

"I'll take that as a 'yes' then," she said.

Jasper stayed in that position for the rest of the journey until we arrived at Tiggy's. I didn't ask him about Rosie. He's allowed to have his own private business too, you know ... But I can imagine in the world of *familiars* he would be considered quite a catch – if you could pin him down.

The front of Tiggy's cottage was well lit, clearing an English lavender bordered path all the way to her front door, only stopping to make way for a small bridge made from driftwood, crossing her waterlily filled pond. She stood waiting on her front porch with whom I could only presume was Rosie, standing next to her with her tail slowly swaying from side to side. Unlike Jasper, her fur was completely white, except for one small black patch around her left ear.

"Welcome and Merry Meet," Tiggy greeted us with arms wide open, embracing us and ushering us into the house. "Make yourselves comfortable. Anywhere you please," she said as she clasped her hands in excitement.

Her sitting room was lined with beach and river landscapes hanging from the walls, and small bowls of collected sea glass and beach treasures filled her shelves and tables. All of her soft furnishings were various shades of dusky blue ... including the carpet. Even though it wasn't my style for an interior, it smelt like freshly baked bread and was warm and inviting.

"I have something for you, Edlynn. I've been so excited to give it to you. Let me put down a saucer of buttermilk for Jasper and Rosie and we'll look at it together."

"Why don't you put your feet up on that ottoman there, Daisy?" Edlynn said, as she relaxed into a single sofa chair. "Give them a rest after the drive. I'm just sorry I can't help in that department. I've tried to learn, but I could never get the hang of it. It hasn't been too much of a hindrance though. There are other ways to get around," she said with a cheeky grin. "Broomsticks are the easiest way to travel incognito. We're free to fly wherever we want. Well, in most places, anyway. Oh, except in the Kingdom of Eswatini, of course, where being caught flying a broomstick above 150 metres will have their traffic officers issuing you a hefty fine."

"A fine? For a broomstick?" I asked.

"It's true," she said. "Look it up."

Tiggy came through to the sitting room carrying a tea tray set for three.

"We don't get to see each other often enough anymore, Edlynn," Tiggy said as she poured the tea.

"I know." Edlynn pursed her lips disappointingly.

"And how is Ailsa?" she asked as she passed Edlynn her cup resting on a saucer.

"Oh, you know Ailsa: always well," she replied.

"You're a friend of Ailsa's?" I asked as she passed me a cup.

She sat down, clasped her hands together and looked at Edlynn. "You didn't tell her?"

"I thought it best that Daisy makes up her own mind," Edlynn said.

"About what?" I asked.

Tiggy looked at me and tilted her head, then tilted it back the other way. "You don't see the resemblance?" she asked.

I couldn't believe I had missed it. I mean, the accent should have been a dead giveaway. But I still wasn't sure. "Are you ... Ailsa's sister?"

"You got it in one guess," she said proudly. "Twins. But as you can see ... not identical."

"Does Ailsa know we're here?" I asked Edlynn.

"There wasn't really the time," she said nonchalantly.

Tiggy adjusted herself in her chair and sipped her tea. "Ailsa hasn't mentioned me, then?"

"Only once," I replied. "She mentioned they assigned you to water magic when we were looking at river maps. She said you didn't speak to each other very often, but also didn't seem to want to talk about it much more. I have to say, Edlynn, I would have preferred you had let me know. It puts me in an awkward position."

Tiggy put her cup down on the table. "There's nothing awkward about it, Daisy. Don't you worry. Your aunt used to visit quite regularly, too."

"She did?"

"Yes. We all hoped that this disagreement would eventually patch itself up, but you know Ailsa ... she can be quite bull-headed. However, I have to say it's also one of her strengths."

"How long has it been since you've spoken?" I asked.

"Well, Daisy ..." – her gaze lingered on the moonlit view out the window – "it's another full moon tonight, and unfortunately, I have lost count of how many more have passed without her."

After spending a few hours with Tiggy, listening to her stories about bargains she had found at trading fairs and traders trying to take her for a fool, I quickly developed a fondness for her. I still had little idea about what happened between her and Ailsa, but it seemed a shame they hadn't been able to work it out. I could imagine Tiggy being a lot of fun to have around. And she obviously shared her love of gardening with Ailsa, even if I could only see her garden in the dark – although much of it was softly illuminated, giving hints at what may lie around the next pebbled path corner. We finished our tea, collected our things, and got ready for the last leg of our journey to the man in the small house.

Edlynn closed the back door of the van and dusted off her hands. "Always a pleasure doing business with you, Tiggy." Edlynn laughed.

I, on the other hand, wasn't so sure I was as happy about the transactions that had taken place over tea and biscuits ... and, more importantly, that I would have to explain all of this to Ailsa.

"Anytime," Tiggy said with a quick bow. "I'll see you in a few hours. Follow the signs to Bagbottom Folly and you'll find your way from there."

Edlynn waved and motioned for me to get in the van, as Jasper sauntered his way over and curled himself up in the cosy woollen blankets on the seat. I closed my door and placed the key in the ignition. "See you in a few hours?" I asked Edlynn.

"I'll explain in a minute," she said as she waved to Tiggy.

We pulled out of her immaculately bordered driveway onto the dark street.

Edlynn adjusted herself in her seat. "I told her we would be back to stay the night before we head back to Folly Gate. We can't very well drive all night. It's not safe."

"Now, Edlynn ..." I said as I kept an eye on the road. "You can't go around organising me all the time. I'm not the little girl you used to see playing at Aunt Olivia's house."

"I know that," she said. "You're a very capable, independent ... *smart ... pretty*—"

"Okay, Edlynn," I said with a gentle smirk. "You don't have to go on. But it's very important that you know I don't need looking after. I am more than capable of doing that myself."

"Have I done something to upset you? I thought you would have been pleased. On such short notice, we could visit the man in the small house, stop off and get a few bits and pieces, say 'hi' to Tiggy and get back in time to open the shop tomorrow. I thought it was a brilliant idea."

"I know your intentions are in the right place, and I have to agree, Tiggy is good company, but please ... in the future ..."

"Understood," she said. "Say no more." She reached across and fumbled through the radio channels until a familiar, nostalgic melody filled the car. She let out a contented sigh, placing her head back against the seat and her hand resting gently on Jasper, as we continued down the road.

"That must be the sign there," I said. "Bagbottom Folly."

We followed the signs until we reached a small gravel road, taking a left at the fork. A large black marker stone sat exactly where it was positioned on the map.

"This must be it," I said. "It should be 400 paces in front of us."

We exited the van, and Edlynn used her wand to illuminate a small narrow path, before pulling her sleeves through her jacket and putting it back on inside out.

"What are you doing?" I asked.

"Pixies ..." she said. "I don't fancy being *glamoured* by them tonight. These woods look like the perfect place for them to play their games and get us lost. It's like a sport to them. You could end up walking in circles for hours."

"Should I turn my jacket?"

"No, I think we'll be fine. I'll lead the way."

"It might have been easier to come during the day," I said.

"We have to get the help we need as soon as possible. We can't have rogue witches running around when the follies are being destroyed. Even if one of those witches could be one of our closest friends."

We continued along the path. "Well, we don't know anything for sure yet. Dawn may be completely unaware. We need proof. Maybe she found the only sour cherry in the bunch. It is certainly not enough to take to Gwendolyn. I dread to think what I might have to do with the proof, if we ever find it."

Edlynn grabbed my arm. "*Water* ... wait."

"Water? There's nothing about water on the map."

Edlynn looked around suspiciously. "Something is not right here. I'll have to take a look."

"What do you mean?" I asked.

"Wait here," she said. "I'll be back in a minute."

I had no longer than flicked my wand and unfolded the map when a whoosh of air passed by me, followed by a slight flash of light. I looked up and found myself staring straight into the eyes of Edlynn, gently bobbing in the air in front of me.

"I told you Tiggy had the best broomsticks in town. This one can really move!" Her eyes widened in excitement.

Jasper jumped up and sat neatly in front of Edlynn. "I never miss a chance to get on a broomstick," he said.

Edlynn tilted the broomstick slightly to the left. "I'll have a look over the water and tell you if I can see anything."

"Take this," I said as I handed her the fae stone. "It's almost midnight."

And in a flash, they were gone, their silhouettes disappearing into the darkness.

I looked down at the map, and I was right. There was nothing about a lake. I looked at Morton's compass, but it was giving no hint as to anything being out of order.

"Daisy …" Edlynn's voice sang across the darkness. "I found it. It's right in the middle of the lake."

Jasper gracefully jumped off the broomstick, and in one swift motion, Edlynn lifted her leg over it as if dismounting a horse, leaving it suspended mid-air in front of us.

"But how are we going to get to it?" I asked.

"Well, I thought you'd never ask," Edlynn replied. "You'll have to jump on. And don't worry, Daisy … I am sure you'll look sweet … upon the seat of a hazel broom built for three," she sang. "Now, tighten your laces!"

CHAPTER TWENTY-FOUR

"**I**'M NOT GETTING ON that thing, Edlynn," I said.

"Oh, come on, Daisy. A witch knows what she needs to know when she needs to know it, right? Just make sure your laces are tight and there'll be no problems. Look at Jasper, not a worry in the world. I promise you it's impossible to fall off."

I paused and looked at her before bending down and tightening my laces. "Just like Em didn't fall off? I'm trusting you, Edlynn."

"Oh, it's not me in charge," she said as I lifted my leg over the back of the broom. "It's our boots!" she yelled as we took off at high speed. It didn't take the broom long before it seemed to settle into the ride. And although our hair was flying back in the wind, there was a silence that enveloped us on the broom.

"It's quiet up here, isn't it?" Edlynn tapped me reassuringly on my leg. "I told you there was nothing to be worried about."

She slipped her hand into her pocket, pulled out the fae stone and looked through it. "There it is," she said as we descended.

I peered over her right shoulder. "I don't see anything."

"Hold on," she said, as we descended and came to an abrupt stop. "Stay close to the broom. I think we are in some sort of field." She looked through the stone. "There it is!"

Edlynn passed me the fae stone, and, as I looked through the small hole, I found it a little hard to believe my eyes. Right there, in front of me, stood a perfectly lit, white thatched cottage: four windows across the top, and three and a door across the bottom. But that wasn't the remarkable thing about this cottage, not at all. The remarkable thing about this house was that it stood no taller than mine or Edlynn's knees.

"You see," Edlynn said, *"the small house."*

"It's certainly not what I was expecting," I said.

Jasper stood unfazed by what stood before us. I'm sure he has seen a lot more than he tells me over a plate of mackerel. The moonlight scattered across each window, but I couldn't see inside the house.

"What shall I do?" I asked Edlynn as I continued looking through the stone. "Ah, wait. I see something." One of the lit windows had a small swinging wooden sign, not dissimilar to something you might see outside an old tavern. A tiny brass bell hung from the sign. "Do you think I should—"

"Go ahead, Daisy," Jasper said. "You're not exactly going to fit through the door."

"You can see the bell?" I asked him.

"Cats are renowned for their night vision," he replied.

I reached up, and pinched the small rope between my fingers and gave a gentle ring. In no time at all, the window snapped open, and a small, well-dressed man appeared. His jet-black hair parted perfectly to the side, wearing a crisp white frilled shirt and a navy-blue blazer. He did the last button up, tugged at the bottom, then swiped his hand across his hair to make sure it was straight before looking directly out at us.

"You can put the stone away," he said. "You should be able to see me as clear as day ... for a short time anyway, so make it quick."

I removed the stone from my eye, and he was right. For such a small man, his abruptness took me aback. "Hello," I said. "I'm Daisy Banks and my friends, Edlynn Cottle and Jasper. We were told you might help us."

A woman's voice came from inside the house, "Not witches again. They bring nothing but trouble. Too much hard work they are."

He waved his hand behind him to shush her. "Witches ... hmm. And from what I can tell ... a *shadow witch*. Well, I don't know what I could possibly help you with. I am the Royal Artist," he proclaimed proudly. "A fine alchemist of the Order. And we all know that means we have little to offer each other – if anything at all."

"A friend ..." I began, "an alchemist himself, said you might be interested in this." I took the bottle Morton had given to me and placed it in front of the house. It stood almost as tall as the front door.

"An alchemist? Friends with a witch? Well, I don't know about that. What's his name?"

"I wouldn't say," I replied.

"Of course you wouldn't," he said.

"He said to tell you it is *Raphael's pigment* and that you would know what that meant."

The woman's voice sounded from inside the house again, "*Raphael's pigment*?" Her voice couldn't hide the delight as she rushed to the window, pushing her husband to the side before dragging him back. "That could come in handy, my lover," she said in her broad West Country accent. "It certainly looks like Raphael's pigment. You haven't opened it, have you? It's highly toxic."

"No. I've brought it to you exactly as he gave it to me. What is Raphael's pigment, if I may ask?"

He looked at me suspiciously before his face softened a little. "The master artist Raphael used it in some of his greatest works. You might have heard of vermilion? Quicksilver-sulphate? Shadow witches are immune to its effects, but should it get into the wrong hands, it could be very dangerous. It's the same compound I used on that painting of your aunt you have hanging in your library ... and it's the reason it is behind crystal glass. You don't want your guests breathing that in."

"You knew my Aunt Olivia?"

"I did. And you're a dead-ringer of her." He leant slightly out of the window. "I have to confess something to you: Morton told me to expect you. I didn't know if I could trust you, though. He assured me ... but alchemists have never found it easy to trust a witch."

"Not all of them are untrustworthy," Edlynn said, a little perturbed by the insult.

"Time will tell," he said to Edlynn. "I see you're not a shadow ... but still lined? You have *the mark* – the small mole behind your ear."

Edlynn brought her hand to her ear and rubbed her finger across it.

He shifted his attention back to me. "I also know you are looking for a crossover potion."

"That's right," I said. "It seems someone is moving through the follies and trying to destroy them. But their magic is messy. I think Aunt Olivia is trying to tell us something, but we can't seem to get a clear message. My coven are all suspects until we can prove otherwise."

"I see," he said. "Then maybe we have a problem that we might help each other with."

"We do? What would that be, then?"

"Yes, maybe we do. *All* crossover potions – well, there's no easy way to say this, as I am the only one with the recipe for it – I am the guardian. The Royal Artist has always kept the recipe hidden in paintings and artworks. But someone must have deciphered the recipe ... *or* taken a copy of mine.

How? I do not know. But, as you can imagine, this does nothing for my reputation or my position as Royal Artist of the Order."

"I see. So, you can help us?"

"Maybe. But we will need something in return … to assure this kind of thing will not happen again. Morton does his best to retrieve any crossover potions he comes across, including counterfeits. He tries to get to every fair he can to keep an eye out. It may help explain his interest in what is happening in the follies to you. But we have never had an unaccounted-for crossover potion … *and* one that works. I usually find any potions that Morton brings are nothing more than useless trinkets. I need all crossover potions returned to me. And the Order wants to know more about the follies – just the maps will do to start with. We have no interest in using them. But crossover potions and follies … we should keep them separate – *and* as quickly as possible. It's a fine line between alchemy and magic. And mixing the two without knowing what you're doing – well, neither witches nor alchemists would be pleased with the outcome, I'm sure. It is why we have tried to keep them separate for centuries."

"I don't think you should try to justify the trials … ever," Edlynn said. "Even if we are in different times. We lost a lot of good witches, and not to mention the lines we lost too."

I paused for a moment, giving them time to settle. I didn't know if I was going to get caught in the middle of a fae fight, but I had my wand ready to snap at any second.

He nodded. "I regrettably agree," he said. "Now, Daisy … do we have a deal?"

"Do you have the crossover potion?" I asked.

He nodded to his wife, who stepped back from the window.

"I see you wear the same sigil as your aunt," he said. "Powerful things they are, if you know how to use them."

"Gwendolyn said it is for protection," I said.

"Protection, yes. But from what? That is the question."

"From what? Don't you mean from whom? I assumed the sigil was unique to my family. Do you know how to use them?" I asked.

"I don't use them myself ... well, not for protection, anyway. Alchemists use symbols to cover what needs to be revealed. But if I was a witch ... a witch that worked with the natural forces of things ... then I might use it to bend the natural forces my way. But how you bend them would be something for you to figure out. Alchemists don't work with magic ... we work with logic ... and rationality – the science of *things and stuff*."

"Things and stuff?"

"Yes, things and stuff. And that *thing* around your neck could probably work with some *stuff*."

"Okay ..." I said as I looked at Edlynn. "What kind of *stuff* do you think this *thing* could work with?"

"Oh, I don't know." He rubbed his forehead. "Most likely to be hidden stuff. If I wanted to use a thing to hide stuff, then the *thing* would probably be some kind of lock. Yes. A *thing* that locks *stuff*."

"Things and stuff," I repeated.

He rested his hands on the windowsill. "You said you thought Olivia was trying to get a message to you?"

"Yes. But I really don't want to say much more about it."

"I understand. But you might want to consider that there was a time when receiving messages from the dead was not so strange. And if you ever want to explore it further, you should ask Morton about his machines."

"Machines?"

"Yes, there have been times throughout history where knowledge and technologies have been lost. And it is one of Morton's areas of expertise. The machines are not of much use to alchemists, besides the odd contraption that helps with our studies, but mix them with magic ... and who knows what you might make them do. Not that we would ever encourage it, of course."

"I'm not sure I'm following. Are you saying that Morton might have a machine that could decipher messages from Aunt Olivia?"

"All I'm saying is, if the crossover potion doesn't suit your needs, maybe magic could use a helping hand from the alchemists. A crossover potion is useless to an alchemist. We can't get them into the follies, anyway. We can only theorise about what might happen. You and Morton may be able to come to some agreement. That's all I'm saying. You might be able to trust Morton more than you think. And he obviously thinks highly of you, otherwise he wouldn't have sent you to me."

The small man's wife appeared back at the window, holding a small bottle. "Be careful with this," he said. "We'll be in touch about the maps." Before passing us the bottle, he held his small hand out, palm up. "The jade first ..."

"Of course," I said and motioned to Edlynn to pay him.

As Edlynn passed the bag of jade coins to him, they seemed to shrink along the way, landing in his tiny hands, and becoming the size of average coins to him. Edlynn noticed my look. "Jade comes in handy for paying fae," she said.

He flicked through the coins, making sure his payment was right. "And the pigment ... you'll have to pass it to me."

I picked up the bottle and, just as with the coins, it became the perfect size to fit neatly into his hand. I had to wonder if it was not really all smoke and mirrors. If alchemists are so against magic ... what I saw happen there looked very much like magic to me.

He passed me a small drawstring bag in exchange. "Your crossover potion. Thank you for your business," he said. "Now, if you don't mind, I'm rather busy."

"I understand," I said. "And thank you."

He closed the small window on the roof of his small house and the lake became dark once again.

"What a nonsense," Edlynn said. "Alchemists are always so smug and think they can make demands. We don't work for them. Remember that."

I motioned for her to keep it down. "We'll talk about it later. We've got to get off this island."

"Well, there's only one way off, Daisy," Edlynn said as she tapped her broom. "On you get! And tighten those laces!"

CHAPTER TWENTY-FIVE

A FTER TRAVELLING BACK ACROSS the lake, safe in the broom's silence, Edlynn carried her broomstick to the opened back door of the van.

"Are you sure you don't want to stop at Tiggy's?" she asked me as she stowed her broom.

"I'm sure," I replied. "I want to talk with Ailsa first. You may have had that conversation with her already, but I haven't, and I think it's the right thing to do ... much to your dismay, I imagine."

We made ourselves comfortable in the van, pulled out of the small clearing, turned onto the road and headed back to Folly Gate.

"Why don't we stop at Bagbottom Folly then, instead?" Edlynn asked. "The sign is coming up shortly. We could see where it takes us and add another folly to your map. We could come with you."

"I think I just want to get that crossover potion back to Folly Gate and into Gwendolyn's hands safely. She can do what she likes with it, but I am hoping she will agree to let us use it to find out what is going on in the follies. Handing it over to her will show her we are as keen as her to find out what is happening. And alchemists seem happy enough to deal with the fae. Maybe with some cooperation, we can somehow figure this out together."

"Fae are always more than happy to play the middleman, but just like the alchemists, it is always for a price ... not to mention their ridiculous games. And as for Gwendolyn, she doesn't even know you have the potion yet," Edlynn said. "And you're perfectly safe with me ... and Jasper, of course."

"I think you've forgotten that I had to go and get Jasper from the folly."

"Well, let's just have a look. We can see if it's worth coming back to investigate later. It will take ten minutes at the most. You can see it from the roadside."

"Maybe you're right, Edlynn. A folly this close to the Royal Artist – it could be worth investigating."

Edlynn sat up a little straighter. "I'm glad you think so," she said with a smile.

We followed the sign into a small tree-covered opening and parked in front of a gate with a wooden step stile to the side, making it easy for ramblers and dog-walkers to enter the field. The ruins of the folly stood directly in front of us.

"Look at the map," Edlynn said. "See if it's showing on there."

I flicked my wand for light and unfolded the map Morton had given me. The folly was marked on the map, but there was no pathway showing where it led.

"Let's have a quick look," I said to Edlynn.

We got out and closed the van doors quietly. The sound softly echoed through the low-lying branches of the tall fir trees surrounding the folly. We heard a branch break behind us.

"It's just me," Jasper said. "I thought I would shift – you know ... just in case."

"Good idea," I said.

We approached the crumbling stone archway. It was larger than usual follies, and a stone turret clung precariously on top of it, leaning slightly to the left, like it could topple at any minute. We looked around the sides of the archway for any symbols or loose stones that could hint at how we would enter the folly.

"I can't see anything. Can you, Edlynn?"

"Not yet," she said as she continued looking.

Jasper stood guarding us as we tried to find a way in. I slid my hands across the rocks on the inside of the archway, left wet from an earlier downpour, finding nothing of significance. Leaning down, I followed a line of yellowed rocks, fitted into the seam of the archway, which ran all the way to the back of it, and before I knew it, *I was in*.

"Edlynn? Jasper?" I called.

Jasper passed through the arch and stood by my side. "Edlynn ..." I called.

"You'll have to come and get me. I'm still in the field. I walked straight through to the other side of the archway."

I reached my hand back through the arch and felt Edlynn's fingertips touch mine, and I pulled her into the folly.

"It looks just like the system in Folly Gate," Edlynn said. "It must be connected."

"There's only one way to find out," I said.

We followed the passage as I swayed my wand left and right to illuminate the cave walls. There was only one direction to move. We had been in there a few short minutes when the familiar exit of the folly entrance to the coast appeared.

"That's a three-hour drive in less than five minutes," I said. "A fast-moving folly? I would say that could be very handy for the right person. We're only a few minutes from Folly Gate." I took out the map. "Look." Edlynn and Jasper leant in. "A new path. A direct line."

Edlynn smiled. "Good work, Daisy. And a much quicker trip to Tiggy's house."

"Maybe next time," I said. "Let's get back." I placed the map back into the side pocket of my bag. "Wait …"

Edlynn and Jasper stopped in their tracks.

"The crossover potion, it's not here."

"What do you mean, it's not here?" Edlynn asked, not hiding her panic. She scrambled through my bag with me, as Jasper growled and surveyed the area. "You must have dropped it somewhere," she said nervously. "We'll just go back the way we came and find it. It can't have just disappeared."

"I'll take the lead," Jasper said.

We walked back along the same passage. Edlynn used her wand alongside mine, but we could find nothing.

"We're never going to be trusted with another potion if we don't find it," I said. "Can you imagine what the Royal Artist will say? It could compromise any dealings we have with the alchemists. And I think they might be the help we need."

Suddenly, an almighty crash brought rocks tumbling down in front of us.

"Not again," I heard Jasper say as we coughed and spluttered, trying to protect ourselves from the dust.

"We'll have to go back," Edlynn said. "We can follow the passage back, come from the other side and keep looking."

"That could take hours," I said.

Edlynn held her hands up in despair. "Well, what do you suggest? We dig our way out?"

Jasper began to remove the rocks from the boulder-choke with his enormous paws. "There's no way to tell how far back the rockpile goes," he said. "But I think we need to get out of here as soon as we can." We turned to head back to the coast entrance when we heard another ear-splitting bang in front of us.

"Another fall! Watch out!" Jasper growled.

"That's it," Edlynn said. "We're trapped. We must be dealing with a *what* rather than a *who*. I didn't see anyone following us."

"We'll figure that out soon enough. But for now, we have to get out of here."

"Here, let me try this," Edlynn said as she raised her wand and struck towards the rockpile. "Just as I thought – nothing. It looks like a cast zone."

"What do you mean?" I asked.

"Don't cast a spell with your wand. We need the light."

"The light?"

"Yes ... the light," she said. She held up her wand, the light emitting from it slowly dulled until it faded completely. "We're dealing with some potent magic here. I'm afraid we'll have to get out the old-fashioned way ... start digging."

I picked up a pointed stone, dug a small hole in the ground and packed my wand into it with dirt, giving us light while we dug.

"It might not take as long as we think," Edlynn said, trying to remain positive, but I could see the panicked determination in her eyes. "I'm not one for small spaces," she added.

Jasper pulled the heavy rocks from the pile, and I rolled them out of the way with Edlynn's help; with each rock we hoped for a glimmer of light. But it was not light that broke through the rock ... but a voice: "*Daisy ... Daisy ... can you hear me?*"

"Gwendolyn?" I yelled through the rocks.

"Yes. Just hold on ... step back and I'll get you out of there."

"Be careful!" Edlynn shouted through cupped hands. "It's a cast zone."

"Step back," Gwendolyn repeated.

The ground under us rumbled and rocks shifted, rolling themselves to the edge of the cave walls until a clear path presented itself. Gwendolyn stood, wand in hand, surrounded by the bright white light emanating from it. "Come on," she said. "Let's get you out of here."

The relentless rain poured down over us as we watched Gwendolyn pace back and forth in front of the folly. We stood, not saying a word. When Gwendolyn eventually stopped pacing and stood in front of us, the rain slid off her skin like water on wax.

"You forgot these," she said as she passed me a small glass box.

"I did?" I looked across at Edlynn as we examined the box holding our alchemists' tools ... *and* the crossover potion.

Gwendolyn stood waiting for an explanation.

"It was my idea," I said. "I wanted the potion to help prove to you it wasn't anyone in my coven that was causing the collapses in the follies. I thought if I could get a crossover potion, we might somehow find out what is causing all this."

"You made these deals without the permission of the High Coven, Daisy."

"I did," I said defiantly.

She took in a deep breath and sighed. We waited for her response. "I tried as well," she said.

Edlynn looked at me. Neither of us could hide the confusion. We waited for her to continue.

"That's how Jasper ended up trapped in the folly. He didn't know what he was carrying, although he thought he did. He has a strong allegiance to us ... and, of course, to you. You are not the only one who has to prove that your witches are not collapsing the follies. I also have superiors to answer to ... and I have little time left. I thought if I followed you, you might find out something I hadn't. So it is not *luck* that I was able to bring you out of the folly. I have been watching you the whole time. And it is not that I don't want your help. In fact, I need your help. I need the help of my witches to secure our place under the Grand Coven. We could lose access to the follies. The Grand Coven could pass them to a new line of witches, which would mean centuries of guardians – our mothers, aunts, grandmothers – would now be for nothing. It would end. But you are a new witch, Daisy, and there are things you don't know, things about your aunt, about your line." She pointed at the glass box. "You didn't even know that you can't take alchemists' tools into follies without protection."

I stood tall in the rain, knowing she was right, and prepared to do whatever it took. "What do we do, High Priestess?" I asked.

Edlynn bowed her head slightly with me in respect. Jasper extended his paw across the ground and bowed, as I had seen him do before.

Gwendolyn held her slender finger to her cheek as she thought. "We find out who is in the follies … *together*. No more secrets. We make a pact between us. We all know a witch's business is her own but, in this matter, there has to be nothing hidden. One of us could hold the answer we need, and we need to know as much as we can sooner than when we need to know it. For instance, the glass box you're holding. It is the only way you can move alchemists' tools through the follies – that we are aware of, anyway. Which means whoever is collapsing the follies also has to have one of those boxes. An alchemist's tool mixed with magic causes the collapses. This kind of thing would have to come from an untutored witch – an *unassigned* witch. Or an even worse thought: there is a coven experimenting with magic which they do not understand. That is something the Grand Coven is sure about. And then there's the matter of using the tools: you have to be able to get them into the folly first. The only person who makes those boxes is the Royal Artist. To be honest, I thought you might have picked

185

one up while you were there, but he let me know you hadn't, which is why I found them easily at the archway entrance. Now ... we have a list ..."

I looked at Gwendolyn. "So ... we are working with the alchemists? I didn't think—"

"Neither did we," Gwendolyn said. "But your aunt tried to convince me to trust Morton. We were trying to form an alliance when she ..."

"I understand," I said.

"I'll explain more later," Gwendolyn continued. "But I think the first thing we have to do is find out who from this list has boxes. However, there's a problem, and the Artist was reluctant to tell me about it. But there are some unaccounted for ... moved through the black market. And I would guess that whoever sold them knows more about who has been moving through the follies."

"But we don't know anything about the black market," I said. "I've certainly never bought anything from a trader."

Edlynn cleared her throat before speaking. "I might know something about that ..." she offered sheepishly.

"Go ahead," Gwendolyn said.

"I would have to ask around," Edlynn said. "But I know someone who might be able to help."

"Good," Gwendolyn said. "Start there."

And with a whoosh of air that parted the rain, she was gone.

I turned to Edlynn. "Who do you know that has anything to do with the black market?"

Edlynn was hesitant to answer. "I know you're not going to like this ... or Ailsa, for that matter. But I think we should take Tiggy up on her offer for a rest."

CHAPTER TWENTY-SIX

I RUBBED MY ARMS as we walked back to the van. The rain began to subside but was still heavy enough to keep everything in its path soaking wet. The needles of the tall standing fir trees dropped collected raindrops across our covered path. Jasper stopped for a moment and shook his coat free of the rain; our feet squelched across the sodden ground. Edlynn turned to Jasper. "Don't worry about being wet," she said. "We'll sort it out when we get in the van."

Jasper shifted. "Less of me to get dry," he said.

I opened the door for Jasper, and he jumped in and curled up on his blanket. I followed him, closed the door and clasped my hands into my chest for warmth. Edlynn drew her wand and tapped the grill of the heater. A fast gush of warm air filled the car, like a velocity dryer at a dependable dog groomer. And almost instantly, the three of us were as dry as if we had never met the rain. I stopped for a moment and turned to Edlynn, keeping my hand on the keys before turning on the ignition. "What did you mean you might know someone that can help?" I asked her.

"I'll explain on the way ... back to Tiggy's," she replied.

I tied my freshly dried hair into a loose bun before starting the van. The tyres of the car crunched passing over the wet ground and snapping twigs, as I reversed and headed back to the main road.

Edlynn picked at some invisible dust from her skirt. "About those brooms we picked up from Tiggy ..." she said.

"Yes," I said as a foreboding feeling passed over me.

"Well ... she never says where they come from. And we never ask. We all know a witch's business is her own. Even after the conversation we had with Gwendolyn, we must respect that."

I glanced at Edlynn curiously. "I thought you weren't one for following the rules," I said.

"I follow the rules ... *mostly*. But you don't always see it. And Tiggy's brooms are the best in the county, the best in the South West even. But it is one reason that Ailsa and Tiggy stopped speaking. She didn't approve of the company that Tiggy always kept. But Tiggy has always been on the right side of the *craft* – even if it means that sometimes she has to be on the wrong side. We all need to be in touch with our shadow sides sometimes. Shadow witches should know that better than anyone."

"What do you mean?"

"I mean, for balance, we need to have good, and we need to have *not-so-good*. And we do the work in order to find that in ourselves – to understand ourselves better. We need to find that balance and accept that we're not *all good ... all the time*. You'll learn more about it as you get deeper into your studies. There may be choices you make which feel like they are not the most moral, shall we say? But we're witches ..."

"And when you figure that out, what do you do with it?" I asked her.

"Well, you're the shadow witch. You will probably be teaching me about *shadow work* in no time."

"Would you say the same thing to anyone ... or only a witch?"

"I think it's important we know ourselves ... all facets of ourselves."

"Would you say that to Thomas, for instance?" I asked. "Is that why you broke up with him – his *shadow side*?"

"I wouldn't put it that way," Edlynn said. "He is one of the few people I have met in my life who seem to be mostly good. But love will do that to a person: we tend to let the shadow side slide. We remember the good times and choose to leave the shadow side buried. But I told Thomas I needed some time ... that *we* needed some time. I need some time to decide what I want. Ailsa's made it clear that she thinks I need to tell him I'm a witch. But, to be honest – and I rarely say this – I'm afraid. I'm afraid that I'm going to lose him. And I would rather not. But it seems I am losing him anyway ... and not through any fault of himself. *Love is never easy* is the strangest statement, yet one of the truest I know. So complicated."

"Wouldn't it be better for you to have the truth out in the open and let Thomas decide?" I asked.

"You would think so, but these things rarely work out, Daisy. In my experience, I haven't ever known it to work. But, times are changing. People are more understanding. Most people are quite happy with a little crystal or tarot shop in their town – somewhere they can go to buy their essential oils and their candles ... and soaps. Some people find them so relaxing, that they look forward to going to a town to visit those kinds of shops ... However, Daisy, I know what you're saying. And maybe you're right. But for now, I told Thomas we need to have some time. I need to have some time to myself."

"I understand," I said as we pulled into Tiggy's driveway. The front light was off, but the curtains were open and a soft light filled the front room.

"Come on Daisy. We'll see what Tiggy has to say and then head back to Folly Gate."

Tiggy greeted us at the door as if she had been expecting us. "Come in. Come in. Thank goodness the rain has slowed," she said as she ushered us inside.

Jasper followed and curled himself up in front of the fire, with Rosie by his side.

"How did it go?" Tiggy asked. "Did you find the folly?"

"We did," Edlynn replied, not at all hiding the fact that she had planned to go there all along. "And we bumped into Gwendolyn."

Tiggy looked surprised. "In the folly?"

"Yes," Edlynn continued. "In fact, she had to get us out of there. It looks like we've got a problem. But I can't discuss very much more about it at the moment. However, there is something you might be able to help us with." Edlynn pulled the small crystal box Gwendolyn had given us out of her basket. "We wanted to know if you've ever seen anything like this."

Tiggy took the box from Edlynn and examined it from the top, the bottom and then peered through the glass sides. "It doesn't seem to be much more than a glass box," she said. "Is there something special about it?"

"It's an alchemist's box." Edlynn looked across at me as if to ask for permission to explain further. I gave her a gentle nod. "It can be used to carry alchemists' tools through the follies."

"I see," Tiggy said. "Well, I see all sorts of trinkets on my travels and through my trading. I think I may have seen boxes similar to this, but I wouldn't have thought anything of it. I simply would have seen them as trinket boxes."

"They could be difficult to distinguish, I suppose," I said. "I imagine they have designed them that way on purpose. Can you remember where you might have seen them?"

Tiggy sat up straight in her chair. "I buy all kinds of knick-knacks at the trading fairs. I would have to think about it."

Edlynn looked across at Tiggy. "We all know they're not exactly trading fairs, Tiggy."

Tiggy shifted uncomfortably in her chair. "I do what is needed ... for the *craft*," she said defensively. "And now that I think about it ... I do remember seeing something like this. And with a few calls, I think I might be able to help you get your hands on one – if that's what you wanted."

I leant forward in my chair. "We're more interested in finding out who the new owners of any of these boxes are. Do you think you could help with that?"

"I'm sure I could find out," Tiggy said, as she passed the box back to Edlynn. "I'll ask around and let you know."

"Thank you, Tiggy," I said.

Tiggy stood up from her chair. "What about some tea ... before you head on back to Folly Gate?"

"That's probably a good idea," I said.

"Good," she said and turned towards the kitchen. "But before I put the kettle on, Daisy ..."

"Yes?" I asked.

"You understand traders are not always ... well, they're not always the most desirable of company."

"I am perfectly aware of what needs to be done," I replied.

Edlynn smirked.

"Good. Then I'll get the tea. Oh, and ..." – she passed me a small jar with some balm in it – "then you can use this after your tea. I picked it up from a travelling trader. It's a refreshing balm. Rub it on your temples and you'll sleep for an hour ... but according to him ... it will feel like ten."

CHAPTER TWENTY-SEVEN

WE LEFT TIGGY'S HOUSE feeling refreshed. The rain pounded against the windscreen of the van, making a rapid drumming sound that lasted most of the journey back to Folly Gate. Ethan was right about the storm and I took caution as he suggested. The relentless weather would last the night, but we arrived safely to the outskirts of town.

"The street lights are out," Edlynn said.

I slowed the van down to make it easier to navigate the narrow country lanes home. "I can't see two feet in front of me," I said.

"Take your time," she said. "Better to arrive late than *dead* on time."

Jasper lay asleep, oblivious to the tension – cats are like that. We continued along the hedge-bordered lanes, their wet leaves glistened under the moonlight.

"Do you think the potion will work?" Edlynn asked. "How do you think it will help us?"

"I'm not entirely sure yet. But it's the only hope we have at the moment."

"Do you know what to expect in the shadows?"

"Who said I was going into the shadows? And anyway, does anybody know what's there?"

"I suppose not. But your determination to find a way to use the crossover potion in the follies only brings me to the conclusion that you are thinking of trying to go there. I really wish Olivia had left some sort of idea about how all of this works."

"I'll do what it takes, Edlynn. And I don't think Aunt Olivia thought she would go to the shadows so soon, otherwise she might have left instructions. And who knows, maybe she has, but we just haven't found them yet."

A bolt of lightning lit up the sky.

Edlynn strained forward to look out through the windscreen. "I think there might be a blackout in Folly Gate. This weather is quite something."

"As long as we get home in one piece," I said as I leant forward too, trying to see better.

Edlynn continued, "I can understand why the follies are so important. You can move around as you please ... regardless of the weather. But nobody really knows what goes on in them. I wonder, though, why there is only a certain line of witches that may move through the follies without permission. Everyone else has to get permission from the High Coven ... or you, as it happens."

"That's why we need to figure it out, Edlynn. Gwendolyn's reputation is on the line too. And I can't imagine who the Grand Coven could replace her with, but I think she is fair. And like she said when we first met, *the Southern Covens look after their witches* ... no matter what line you come from, or what level you are, or even what coven you belong to. If we have something moving across from the shadows, or someone moving freely through the shadows, then we should know who they are and what they're up to. Maybe this is why the Grand Coven is so strict about monitoring trade. But until the follies are mapped correctly, they are of little use to anyone, I suppose. I am sure Aunt Olivia must have mapped a lot more than the few paths I have on my maps."

"I'm not sure how interested the Grand Coven are about trade. But trade is one reason Ailsa and Tiggy fell out. Tiggy has always had some brilliant jade trades ... but they may not have always come from the most reputable sources. And she never lets anyone know where she gets them. And we know our Ailsa likes to keep her nose clean, by the book and in the old ways."

We were about to drive past Thomas's house when Edlynn asked me to stop the van.

"What for?" I asked. "It's the middle of the night."

"Thomas's lights are off ..."

I slowed the car down and looked at Edlynn. "I suspect that may be because it's the middle of the night."

"He always leaves his porch light on ..."

"The storm must have taken out his electric, that's all."

"Turn your headlights off," she said. "I just want to make sure he's okay."

I pulled up on the street verge at the front of his house and reluctantly turned the engine off. "I don't feel right about sneaking around his house at this hour," I said.

We quietly opened our car doors. Jasper remained sleeping as Edlynn hushed me and waved her hand to follow.

"I'll just peek through and see if he's okay," she said.

"I don't like this, Edlynn ..."

"It will only take a minute and I'll know he's all right."

"I thought you two had broken up," I said as I followed her, hunched over and trying to protect my vision from the rain.

"This is his sitting room," Edlynn said. "I'll just have a quick look and we'll go."

A large puddle had formed underneath the window, but that didn't stop Edlynn. She gently lifted her feet about 12 inches off the ground and peeked through the window. "There's a lantern on in there," she said.

"Right," I said. "Now come down and leave the man alone. He's obviously fine and just has no electric like most of Folly Gate, I expect."

"I'll just check around the back. I mean, why would he leave a lantern unattended?"

I tried to convince her to leave, but she kept her two feet five inches off the sodden ground and headed to the back of Thomas's house. She found another window and floated herself up. "He's not in his kitchen ..." Edlynn whispered.

"All right ... let's—"

A voice from behind interrupted me, "Edlynn? Daisy? Why are you peeking through my kitchen window?"

Edlynn dropped to the ground. The mud splashing up over her boots. "Thomas ... I—"

Thomas stood in front of us, holding a lantern, and wiped the wet hair from his face. "I know what you were doing, and I know what I saw."

"Thomas, you're bleeding," I said.

He moved uncomfortably and wiped his forehead, inspecting the blood under the lantern. "So I am," he said. Bonnie, his black and white Border Collie, came steaming out of the bushes and skidded to his side.

"I had a fall ... It's nothing to worry about," Thomas said. "The electrics of this old house are underneath it, in the cellar. I was checking down the stairs and must have missed my step."

"I think everyone's electric is out," I said.

Edlynn stepped towards Thomas. "Well, let's get you out of this rain and get your face cleaned up. It looks like a nasty cut."

Thomas looked at us suspiciously. "Well, I suppose as we're all awake now, I may as well put on a pot of tea. Come on, let's get out of this weather." We followed him up to the back door as my side glances at Edlynn were lost in the dark. "I've got the coal stove going," he said. "We can make tea on there." He stepped out of his country boots, and we followed suit, slipping our muddy boots off and leaving them by the back door.

"Why don't I put the tea on?" I offered. "And Edlynn, you can attend to Thomas's wound …"

But before we could move, Thomas stopped us. "I saw you, Edlynn," he said.

"I know," she replied. "I'm sorry. I put Daisy up to it. We were driving back, and I wanted to make sure you were all right."

Thomas shifted his weight as he slid off his tan leather gloves. "No, Edlynn. I mean … I saw you … *floating*."

Edlynn's face flickered with fear for a split moment before she cleared her throat and said, "Oh dear, Thomas. You really have hit your head. *Floating* … you said? Of all the absurd things …"

"I know what I saw," he continued. "Daisy? You must have seen it, too."

"I … I … can't say I did, Thomas. I'm sorry. Why don't you sit down and let us deal with that nasty cut?"

Thomas pulled out a handkerchief from his pocket and placed it on his forehead. "Why won't you tell me the truth, Edlynn?" Thomas asked. "I've stepped back and done everything you have asked of me. The last few weeks have been … well …"

"All right, Thomas." Edlynn patted his arm. "We'll talk about this later."

"The first-aid box is under the sink," Thomas said to me as he resigned himself to his chair.

Edlynn nodded at me to fetch the box.

When I returned, it had become apparent Thomas was not going to let the issue go. He rested his head back against the chair in frustration. "Edlynn, I know that a witch's business is her own ..."

Edlynn tried hard to cover her gasp. "What do you mean?" she asked, holding his gaze.

"Olivia told me ..."

"Olivia told you what?" she asked him, as I passed her the first-aid box.

He raised his arms in defeat. "The day she signed her will, leaving everything to Daisy. She gave me firm instructions not to contact Daisy until at least four weeks after her funeral ... *and* ... she told me ... she told me she was a witch. She said there were more witches about, and that's why she didn't want Daisy notified about her funeral – in case there was any trouble."

Edlynn overdramatised her confused look. "Trouble? And what do you mean, she was a witch?"

"Oh, Edlynn," he said. "Why won't you tell me the truth?"

"There's nothing to tell, Thomas." Her eyes welled in her pleas of ignorance. "I have no idea what Olivia—"

Quiet whimpers from Bonnie interrupted her. The bedraggled dog stood to our side, the light of the coal fire catching her silhouette, with her right paw lifted in the air.

"She must be hurt." Thomas groaned and clutched his rib as he tried to get up out of his chair.

Edlynn instinctively grabbed his elbow to support him.

"I'm okay ... I'm okay," he said to her and gently limped towards his injured friend. We watched as he squatted down and cupped her muzzle in his hands before kissing her forehead and taking her paw. As he rubbed her wet muddy paw, checking for injury, he leant down and whispered to her, "You did well, my Bonnie girl ... you did well."

CHAPTER TWENTY-EIGHT

A WITCH'S BUSINESS IS her own – and I intended on holding myself to that as I drove Edlynn home. However, it didn't stop me from thinking about what Thomas had said, and especially what he had said to Bonnie. Ailsa had warned Edlynn time and time again that eventually she would have to tell Thomas the truth, and it seemed like she had let the perfect opportunity to do that slip through her fingers. As I pulled into Edlynn's driveway, I couldn't help but think that, not only was Edlynn hiding something from Thomas ... but Thomas was also hiding something from us.

"Why don't you come in for a cup of tea?" Edlynn asked as the van came to a stop. "I expect you have questions about why I didn't tell Thomas everything."

I sensed her discomfort. "Thanks for the offer, Edlynn, but it's been a long night and I think I'll leave you to get some rest."

Edlynn agreed with a slight tilt of her head. "Well, remember that the refreshing balm will last as long as you want it to ... but when you do eventually sleep, you won't wake for 10 hours. A little lavender on your pillow will subdue its effects."

I smiled gently at her as she stepped out of the van. "And whatever is between you and Thomas stays between you and Thomas. But I hope you can work it out. And you can let me know all about it when you do."

"I will," she said as she flipped the seat forward, reached back and picked up her basket. She gave Jasper a quick scratch behind his ears. "Hopefully we hear from Tiggy soon."

"Let's get some rest," I said. "We'll open the shop later today."

I waited until Edlynn gave a quick wave from her front door before heading home, and continued to wonder what really happened with Thomas. The injury to his head looked more like a scratch to me. But I suppose a loose piece of wood sticking out from somewhere, or a low-lying beam in the cellar, could do that. Did Bonnie try to save him from a fall? Or was there something else going on? And why would Aunt Olivia disclose to him she was a witch? But, I suppose, *we can't forget*, a witch's business is her own, and if she wanted to tell him that ... then *so mote it be*. Maybe I was over-thinking the situation and simply needed some rest.

As I pulled into my drive, I felt the questions slow down in my mind, and the sound of my front door opening welcomed me home. I went to step over the threshold and noticed a small package on the floor which had been popped through the letter box in my door. As I bent down to retrieve it, I recognised Ethan's handwriting. Jasper followed me through to the kitchen, where I filled his water bowl before reading the note.

The note, written on Folly Gate Constabulary stationery, was folded into quarters with a rubber band securing a USB stick inside.

Daisy,

I didn't want to wake you. These are the files sent over by the videographer from Kate's party. I have to get to Exeter and hope you might be able to take a look at them. I'll be in touch later in the day.

Thanks for your help,

Ethan

"Well, it looks like the rest will have to wait, Jasper," I said. "I'm going to freshen up and I'll be down to make you some breakfast."

"No rush," he said. "It's still a little early for me."

I went to make my way up the stairs when Em popped her head out of her room, her eyes squinting at me and her hair tangled like a wild bramble bush. "Have you been back in those follies? I hope not. You could have been stuck in there longer than overnight …"

"Everything is fine, Em," I replied. "Go back to sleep. We'll have some breakfast later."

She huffed and closed her door, reminding me of one of those cranky old landladies who doesn't appreciate the slightest disturbance from her tenants.

I stepped into my bathroom, relying on my wand to give me the quick freshen-up I needed. The scent of jasmine filled the room every time I came in there now, like a default aroma in the air. Maybe it was a remnant of a spell from Aunt Olivia, but I had no intention of changing it.

A plush robe covered my shoulders and enveloped me in its warmth, before tying its belt gently around me and finishing with a neat bow. I slipped my feet into the pair of fluffy lined slippers and headed back downstairs.

Jasper was waiting in the sitting room, having already found himself a cosy cushion on the sofa. I sat down next to him and opened my laptop. "Let's see if we can find the evidence we need, Jasper."

The videographer must have had at least three cameras, as far as I could tell at first glance. I opened the file labelled 'Arrivals' and sped up the footage.

Jasper moved over towards me. "An extra pair of eyes," he said. "Oh, there you are going up the gangway …"

"You would have loved it, Jasper. Definitely your kind of party."

"But what would I wear to such a grand occasion?" he said, not disguising his over-dramatic response.

I laughed. "I'm sure Edlynn would have found the perfect outfit for you." We continued to study the footage. "Well, there doesn't seem to be anything unusual there," I concluded. "Let's try another file ... and then we'll take a breakfast break."

The videographer captured the night and its ambiance with absolute professionalism. Laughing guests and slow-motion clips across the tables brought back the recent memories of what I, alongside most of the other guests, thought was a more than successful evening: a party that would be talked about for years to come.

"You have some moves," Jasper teased, as the sped-up footage of me with Edlynn and Dawn on the dance floor played.

"Ah, this is where I went for some fresh air ... and then I came back in here ... Ben was ... hold on ... Amie is passing him something ..." I zoomed in. "It's the bottle of prosecco he was drinking from when Ellie was trying to get him to have coffee. You see, Jasper? I can't make out if it is one of the bottles I brought for Kate ... Then she goes and sits quietly on the edge of the room there ... Why would she encourage him to drink more? She told me he got like that sometimes ... I told you there was something about Amie. I think I better get hold of Ethan."

I picked up my phone and called Ethan, but it went straight to voicemail. "Ethan. It's Daisy. I found something in the files. Call me as soon as you can." I flipped my laptop shut and kicked off my slippers. "No time for rest yet, Jasper. We're taking a drive to the Folly View Hotel."

I drove through the back alleys that ran along behind *Liv's Lumières* and headed straight towards the Folly View Hotel.

"Rubbish day!" I exclaimed.

"Well, I don't think the weather has had a chance to show itself yet," Jasper replied.

"Not the weather, Jasper …" I said as I came to a hard stop at the back of the shop. I pulled the handbrake up and left the engine running, as I ran to bring the shop's bins to the kerbside.

"Oh … *rubbish day.*" Jasper chuckled.

"I don't want overflowing bins for the next week," I said. "Edlynn said it's impossible to get a collection if we miss it." I pushed down on the handbrake and continued up the alleyway.

"What's the rush?" Jasper asked. "You can hardly arrest Amie without Ethan there."

"I'm not looking to arrest her, Jasper. I merely intend to stall her until I can get a hold of Ethan."

"Why not try the Sarge?"

"And tell him what? I saw Amie pass Ben a drink at the party. I'm not even sure Ethan will be able to do anything about it."

"So, what's the point of going to see Amie?"

"All I know is a witch knows what she needs to know when she needs to know it. And I can't explain it, but I'm certain I am meant to know that Amie passed Ben a drink – as insignificant as it may be to the case."

We pulled into a car space closest to the entrance of the hotel; the soft chittering of the morning songbirds followed us as we crossed the car park. I stopped and looked down at Jasper as we reached the base of the stairs.

"You go and get her, Daisy," he said. "I'll be waiting right here."

"Get in the van, Jasper! Get in the van!" I yelled as I ran down the hotel stairs.

Without hesitation, he turned and ran, keeping up with me as we headed towards the car.

"What's going on?" Jasper asked as he jumped into the front seat.

"Amie has checked out of the hotel – earlier this morning. And Ellie is no longer in the Penthouse. We have to get to Kate's house." I reached for my phone and called Ethan again. "Come on, Ethan. Answer your phone ..." But I was met with the now familiar 'You've reached the phone of D.C. Fairfield. I'm unavailable right now but please leave a message ...' I waited for the tone. "Ethan. It's Daisy again. Amie has checked out of the Folly View Hotel. I'm heading to Kate's. Call me as soon as you get this message."

I left a stream of dust behind the van as we screeched away from the hotel and began *rat-running* through the back roads of Folly Gate.

"Go left here," Jasper said. "You can cut through after the florist on the right."

I followed Jasper's directions out of Folly Gate and down onto the lane that would take us to Kate's house.

"Do you think Amie will be at Kate's?" Jasper asked.

"I'm hoping so, and then I can stall her there until I hear from Ethan. We have to appear calm and collected when we arrive."

"Well, take a few deep breaths then, Daisy. I can hear your heart rate from here."

"You're right," I said, as we turned into Kate's bumpy drive, and took in a long, deep breath through my nose and let it out of my mouth.

"Slow down ..." Jasper said, as his head jerked left and right. "I think you've hit every pothole ..."

"We're taking a page from Ethan's handbook," I said. "A false sense of security ... then sweep in with the evidence. Are you coming in?" I asked him as I pulled up.

"I wouldn't miss it."

We stood at Kate's front door for a moment as I straightened myself out and looked down at Jasper. "Ready? Remember, we have to appear calm."

Jasper sat neatly by my side ... and I pressed the doorbell.

Kate answered the door dressed in her pyjamas, her hair was tied back in a ponytail, and her skin looked freshly cleaned. She held a flute of champagne in her hand and seemed unsurprised by my arrival. "Daisy ... come in. You probably think it's a bit early for champagne. But after everything we've been through ... well ... follow me through. Ellie's in the kitchen. You're more than welcome to join us. One more for champagne, Ellie," she sang as we followed her.

Ellie poured a glass for me and replaced the bottle to its ice bucket. "There you are, Daisy," she said. "We were just about to toast."

"Wow," I said. "This is quite a spread for breakfast."

Ellie pulled out a stool for me at the kitchen bench, laden with scones, croissants, a fresh fruit platter and a box filled with chocolate brioches. Kate placed a small plate in front of me. "There's plenty. Help yourself."

I placed a croissant on my plate. "You must have been up early to get all this ready."

"Well, I'm an early bird anyway," Kate said, "but it wasn't me. It was Amie. She left a note and said she was heading back to London early and didn't want to disturb us, but hoped we would enjoy a parting gift. Breakfast was all set up, ready for us, when we came downstairs."

"Amie?" I asked. "She's already left?"

"Yes. She's catching the Southern Angel steam train this morning."

"The Southern Angel? We have to find out what time it leaves."

Ellie looked at me, confused. "Is everything all right, Daisy?"

I turned the bottle in the ice bucket and recognised the label. "This is prosecco ..."

Kate leant in to read the label. "Oh, so it is."

"It's one of the bottles I gave you as a gift," I said.

"Oh," Kate sounded surprised. "Why would Amie do that? I haven't had a chance to go through all my gifts yet. There's been so much going on and—"

"Was this bottle opened when you came down?" I asked them.

"Yes," Ellie said. "It was in the ice bucket with a stopper in it. What's going on, Daisy? You have to tell us."

"It's Amie," I said. "I was hoping she would be here. We have to get her off that train. I think she is involved in the captain's death ... and" – I looked at Ellie – "Ben's."

"Amie?" Ellie looked down and shook her head. "Amie wouldn't do something like this."

"I'm sorry, Ellie, but the evidence is saying something different. I have to stop her so we can be sure. Don't touch anything here. Especially the prosecco."

"How will you stop her?" Ellie asked.

"Do you know what time the Southern Angel is leaving?" I asked.

"I can look it up," Kate said.

"No, we're wasting time. I'll drive straight to the station now."

Ellie was making her way out of the kitchen. "If Amie had anything to do this with, I want to hear the words come from her mouth. I'm coming with you, Daisy."

"Me too," Kate said, as she rushed after her sister.

"I'll get the van started," I said. "Come on, Jasper. Breakfast will have to wait."

CHAPTER TWENTY-NINE

I TURNED OVER THE ignition and tooted the horn. "Come on. Let's go," I said under my breath and grabbed my phone to call Ethan again. But there was still no answer. "Ethan. It's Daisy ... again. I really wish you would get back to me. Amie is taking the Southern Angel train. I'm with Kate and Ellie and we're headed to the station now. Call me as soon as you can."

I leant over Jasper and pushed the passenger door open as Ellie ran to the car with Kate close behind her. Ellie slid into the middle of the bench-seat and handed Jasper to Kate.

"Hold on to him tight," I said.

"I will. I promise," Kate replied as she adjusted herself and slammed the door shut. "Okay, let's go!"

I handed Ellie my phone. "Hold this. I'm expecting a call."

The van bounced along Kate's driveway before we pulled out onto the single-tracked road towards Folly Gate station.

I tapped my fingers impatiently on the steering wheel as we drove up behind a tractor, its wide wheels clipping uncut bramble as they extended to the edges of the country lane.

"There's a passing place just ahead," Kate said.

The farmer pulled in slowly to the side of the road and waved us around. I lifted my hand in a casual *thank you* and brought my focus back to the task at hand.

We were less than minutes from the train station when we noticed plumes of white smoke drifting along the treetops.

"We've missed it," Kate said. "It's already left."

I opened my window and, as if on cue, its loud whistle blew, followed by the *chug-chug-chugging* of the Southern Angel steam train.

"We'll get ahead of it," I said. "Which way?"

Kate pointed out the window. "Turn right up here. The road to my vet runs along the train line. But I think the train is *express* through the next station."

We lost sight of the grand Southern Angel steam train for a short while, as we passed the last of the farms on the outskirts of town, and crossed a single-lane stone bridge before turning a corner, just in time to see the gate of the level-crossing lowering.

"We won't make that," Ellie said.

I slowed down. "Don't worry, Ellie. I'm not going to try. But maybe we should put our heads down – in case she is looking out the window. We don't want to give her a *heads-up* that we're on the way."

"Hah," I heard Jasper chuckle. "Good one, Daisy. *One is amused.*"

I glanced across at him as the train passed the crossing. We sat waiting for the gate to lift when my phone rang. Ellie tilted the screen towards me. "Answer that," I said as I pulled through the crossing. "And put it on speaker ..."

"Daisy," Ethan's voice came through my phone.

"*Ethan.* Where have you been? I've been trying—"

"At the hospital—"

"The hospital? Are you okay?"

208

"Yes, perfectly fine, but I had to switch my phone off. It's not important now. I'll explain later but ... Daisy ... you were right – right about every-thing. The Sarge has executed a warrant for Amie's arrest."

"He has? That was quick," I said. "Well, she's on the Southern Angel. We missed her at the Folly Gate station. But we're following her now."

"You are? Well, where are you?"

"Almost at St Michael's station. But Kate seems to think the train doesn't stop there."

"Keep following it," Ethan said. "I'll get them to hold the train at Brack-en station. I'm on my way back from Exeter. Get to the station and stall Amie. I'll make sure the Sarge isn't far behind."

***

The Southern Angel sat nestled in the station as we arrived.

"*Ugh*," I said. "Typical ... no parking." I pulled into the *kiss-and-ride*.

"You can't park there ..." I heard someone yell, as we got out of the van and ran towards the platform. Kate and Ellie followed me, with Jasper close at my heels. "I wonder what they'll say to the pile of police cars about to arrive," I said under my breath.

An announcement came over the platform: "The Southern Angel is currently experiencing a delay due to an obstruction on the track. We apologise for any inconvenience and service will resume as soon as possible. We would ask that all passengers please remain on board."

I peered through the window of the last carriage. "Can you see her?"

"No," they answered in unison.

"Keep looking," I said, stating the obvious.

A woman scooped up an on-the-run toddler ahead of us, before stepping back from the yellow line and waving and blowing kisses to a leaving passenger. Kate and Ellie ran ahead of me as I leant down to pick up Jasper. "Best not to take any chances," I whispered into his ear.

"She's here!" Ellie cried. "In the compartment carriage ..."

"You take the door ahead and I'll take this one," I shouted as I jumped on board – being careful to *mind the gap*.

I searched from one direction as I watched Kate and Ellie pressing their hands up against the windows of each compartment in search of their *friend*.

"I have her," I said, as I slid back the compartment door.

Amie sat with an empty teacup on her side table and an unopened packet of ginger biscuits. She stood up.

"Daisy." She smiled. "I didn't know you were on the train."

Ellie stepped in front of the door. "Well, we knew you were," she said as they locked eyes.

Amie held her smile. "Oh, and Kate's here too. You're welcome to join me. I have the compartment to myself. I could get us some tea."

I stepped closer to her, still clasping Jasper, allowing Kate to block the door as Ellie stepped into the vintage compartment.

"There's nowhere to run, Amie," I said. "You won't make it off the platform. We know everything. I have seen you pass Ben the poisoned prosecco with my own two eyes. And as for the hemlock ... you were quite smart to consider hiding it in the quail, but you forgot one thing: it's the wrong time of the year. In the autumn, you may well have gotten away with it ... but certainly *not* in the spring. A small oversight, perhaps, but one that let me know the hemlock had to have come from somewhere else. And as we have now discovered, that *somewhere else* was in fact you. The police are on their way and will arrive any second now. In fact, I think I hear their sirens. But while we wait ..." – I took a step closer to Amie – "Kate and Ellie deserve to know why you killed Ben."

Amie looked at her 'friends'. Her expression showed no signs of panic or remorse. She stood as if everything was exactly as she wanted it to be.

Ellie couldn't hold the silence, "How could you, Amie?" she asked through her tears.

Amie's demeanour changed. "It's *always* all about you. Isn't it, Ellie?" she snarled. "And Kate, you know you're not much better."

Kate answered her, "We have no idea what you're talking about, Amie. We have always stood by you – and through the hardest of times."

Amie stiffened her shoulders and held her head high. "I think you'll find I was the one that stood by the both of *you*. When your parents died, and you inherited all that money, you moved away and left me with nothing – discarded me. We were like sisters. Well, at least that's what you wanted me to believe. But when it came down to it, I was nothing but a third wheel. And when Ben broke up with me, I left for India – to find myself, to live *my* life. Not a life that revolved around the two of you. But when I came back ... well, you had taken him from me too."

"Are you talking about Ben?" Ellie asked.

Amie became enraged. "Of course, I'm talking about Ben! You knew I loved him. Do you honestly think he loved you, Ellie? I did you a favour – believe me. He was only after your money, Ellie. And he discarded *me* for a chance to take it from you."

"That's not true, Amie, and you know it. Ben had some issues, it's true, and they weren't easy to deal with, but you had been gone for a year before anything happened between us."

Amie's eyes went cold. "You broke the *girl code*, Ellie. I always knew you wanted Ben. It was obvious – *written* all over your face."

"I never—"

"Save it, Ellie," Amie said. "I've heard enough from you."

"And what about the captain?" Kate asked.

Amie's eyes lit up. "I didn't intend for that to happen. But Ben didn't eat his quail. He gave it to the captain, so I had to find another way."

"The captain ate Ben's quail?" I asked.

"Every last bit of it," Amie answered.

I continued to question her, "How did you know Ben would order the quail in the first place?"

Amie looked at Kate and Ellie with delight as she seized her ultimate moment of glory, bathing in their pain. "He always ordered the most expensive thing on the menu. Something I learned about him when we were dating. He was such a walking cliché. And Kate, when you agreed to let me take care of the catering, I made sure quail was at the top of the menu – the perfect cover for a hemlock poisoning. I made a point of letting him know the quail was the most expensive meal earlier in the evening. And all that was left for me to do was to take a little *trip* over my foot behind his chair, and a joke about my lack of *sea legs*. It was the perfect moment to slip the hemlock into his meal. But when I saw he hadn't eaten the quail, I had to think quick, so I handed him the bottle of prosecco. But Ellie tried to take it from him, and it spilled across the floor. However, I wasn't going to let you win, and offered you a hangover cure for him instead. *And ...*" – she dusted her hands – "my work was done. You should be grateful, Ellie. I've saved you years of heartache. Years that I have had to endure myself, because of him."

"Grateful!" Ellie exclaimed. "We were engaged, Amie. I loved him." She held her hand across her forehead. "The dropper bottle ..." she said. "And I insisted he tried it. Oh, Amie. What have you done?"

Amie smirked. "Maybe in the future you will pay a little more attention to what is going on in other people's lives."

"But why would you take Kate down, too?" Ellie asked. "She has done nothing to hurt you ... ever."

"Well, that was a necessity. And I'm sure you'll find out in good time." Amie pointed outside the carriage towards the Sarge running across the platform, followed by three officers heading our way.

Kate stepped to the corridor window and waved them over as Ellie made her way to a corner of the compartment. "I'm not missing this," she said.

I nodded and made my way into the corridor of the carriage as the Sarge boarded and motioned for two of the officers to cuff Amie. Ellie breathed deeply and didn't take her eyes off Amie. The officers placed Amie's hands in front of her, clicked the handcuffs and escorted her out of the train. I followed behind them towards the Sarge.

"We got her, Sarge," I said.

He extended his hand out to me. "I've said this before to your aunt. She always managed to be in the right place at the right time. And now it seems the torch may have been passed onto you. Good work, Daisy," he said, as he clasped my hand. "We'll take it from here."

CHAPTER THIRTY

I WALKED BESIDE KATE and Ellie as they consoled each other out of the station. Jasper remained in my arms. Ethan was speaking to the officer that had arrested Amie when he saw us and waved, before making a gentle jog our way.

"You did it, Dais'," he said.

"We did," I replied and looked across at Kate and Ellie.

Ethan stepped closer. "You were right about everything. The dropper bottles taken from Kate's house contained hemlock. Amie wasn't taking any chances."

"I knew it," I said. "When I saw the bottles Kate had, I recognised them from Amie's handbag when she was in my shop ... and then to see another similar bottle at Ben and Ellie's ... I had to look into it further. I wouldn't be an investigator if I didn't."

Ethan grinned. "Well, your hunch was right about the gardens, too. The Sarge took it seriously and was able to get a hold of the Head Gardener. It didn't take long for him to find out what had happened. Apparently, Amie had been able to sweet talk her way into a private tour of the poison gardens with one of their new employees, presenting her with the perfect opportunity to get her hands on some hemlock."

"Well, Ethan, you have the *opportunity* sorted, and I think you'll find we have a pretty clear motive. Amie couldn't help but spill every detail of her work to Kate and Ellie. They say killers like to keep a trophy ... Amie's trophy was the despair on Kate and Ellie's faces as she told them how she carried out her plan for revenge."

"We'll have to take statements as soon as we can."

"Of course," I said. "Well, you made it back just in time. I hope everything was okay at the hospital."

"It will be. I went for breakfast with Dad at the hospital, and they didn't allow phones in Mum's ward. We try to make things as normal as we can for her."

"I understand."

"But, as I was in Exeter early, it gave me the chance to speed up the results on the bottles. And before I knew it, the Sarge had executed a warrant – which reminds me, your friend's prosecco ... it's perfectly safe, as long as no one opened it at the party. But I would like to take the other bottles from Kate into evidence."

"Well, I think Kate may have seen enough prosecco for a while. And maybe I have too."

"That would be completely justified," he said.

"Oh, and I found some more evidence you may be interested in – from the videographer, it sent me looking for Amie. I'll get Kate and Ellie home and bring it to you later."

We paused as we watched Amie being driven away. Her eyes never left the sisters, and the lights of the police car flashed as they left the station. Kate pulled Ellie into an embrace.

"I'll speak to them," Ethan said as he placed a gentle hand on my shoulder to follow him.

Ellie stepped towards us. "Thank you, Daisy. I dread to think what might have happened if you hadn't turned up so early. If Daisy hadn't arrived when she did, Ethan, we may well have been Amie's next victims."

"Amie had left them a less than well-intentioned breakfast," I said. "You might want to send a team to collect it."

"I'll get one there straightaway," Ethan replied.

"Well, we got her," I said as I looked at Kate and Ellie. "And now Folly Gate constabulary will take over."

Ethan removed his hat. "We still have some investigations to make – some loose ends to tie up – but I can assure you we will present the best case we can."

"Thank you." Kate let out a sigh.

"Well, maybe I should get you both home," I offered.

Ethan agreed, "Yes, there's not much more you can do for now. Don't touch anything from your breakfast. I'll make some calls and head straight to you. We'll try to get a team in and out of there as quickly as we can, so you can get some rest. If you need anything you have my number."

I pressed my key fob as the sisters turned towards the van. "It's open."

"Call me later today," Ethan said. "We can organise anything we need to then."

"Will do." I placed Jasper on the ground and made my way to the van.

"Oh, and Daisy ..." Ethan's voice came from behind me.

"Yes?"

"Good work," he said. "We're lucky to have you working with us."

"Lucky?" I asked under my breath.

Hmm ... I think I'll let that one slide ...

Kate passed Jasper over to me and opened her door.

"Would you like me to wait with you until Ethan arrives?" I asked her.

"Thanks," she replied. "But we'll be okay. He shouldn't be long, and with Amie in handcuffs ... well, I'm sure we have nothing to worry about." She helped Ellie out of the van. "We wouldn't have caught her without you, Daisy. We were one toast away from being Amie's next victims."

"Well ..." I began, "maybe when this is all over, you will let me invite you for a proper breakfast – just the three of us. I'll cook."

"We would love that," Kate said, as she closed the door.

I waited for a moment as their arm-linked figures disappeared in my rear-view mirror before driving home.

"Breakfast sounds nice," Jasper said as we pulled into our street. "Especially if you're cooking ... *for them*."

"Yes," I said. "Thank you, Jasper. I've seen Edlynn put on some splendid breakfasts. Maybe it's time for me to start *wanding* up some culinary delights."

"Maybe it is." Jasper chuckled. "But I think you have forgotten one thing."

"What's that?"

"What will *you* eat?"

"Well, whatever I *wand,*" – I tsked out aloud – "*shadow food.*"

"Exactly. You know you've never actually tasted your own wanded food, Daisy. Maybe you're lucky, and it's skipped a generation."

I glanced across at Jasper. "One thing I know, Jasper, is that shadow magic *never* relies on luck."

"Yes, my witch."

"Maybe we'll wand up some shadow food when we get in," I said with a wink. "I know you're only trying to help."

"Of course."

Our chat was interrupted when we pulled into our driveway and caught sight of Amber running out of the front door towards us, with Em close behind.

"Daisy! Daisy! Come quickly!" Amber planted her hands on my open window before opening my door.

I stepped out and took her by the shoulders. "Amber ... take a breath. What is it?"

She composed herself. "The Prime Spell Book ... We didn't do anything to it, I swear. It just ... Well, follow me. See for yourself."

I flung my bag across the kitchen bench as I scurried after her, leaving Em and Jasper in my wake. Upon reaching the library door, Amber took a step back and motioned for me to enter.

"Look," she said.

Scarlet stood next to the Prime Spell Book, her wand poised to take on anyone who might enter. "I found it like this when I came to read," she said, as she lowered her wand. "It hasn't changed since – just more blank pages."

I stepped towards the lectern. The Prime Spell Book lay open, lit by a soft lilac light that pulsated as if breathing in a light slumber.

"They're not blank pages," I said, as I tried to make sense of what I was seeing.

"They're not?" Scarlet asked and looked again.

Amber and Em came closer and agreed with Scarlet.

"We can't see anything," Em said.

"It looks like some sort of riddle," I said.

Em looked closer. "A riddle? There's nothing there ..."

"There is." I read aloud:

> *"The key you need is in the air.*
> *The sign you hold will take you there."*

Our heads shot to the ceiling and we roved the room with our eyes.

Amber grabbed the air with her hand. "I don't see any keys."

"It might not be an actual key," Scarlet said.

Em petted her mouse sitting neatly in her blazer pocket. "Well, if it's not an actual key ... then maybe we could figure out what *sign* you might be holding, Daisy."

"I don't know," I said as I patted down my skirt. "Do you see anything on me?"

Amber stepped in to help, checking my collars and cuffs. "Nothing there."

Scarlet reached for my neck, but I grabbed her arm before she could touch it. "It's okay," she said as she slowly dragged out my necklace hidden away underneath my blouse. "Your sigil ..."

"My sigil?" I looked down at the amulet Gwendolyn had given me in this library in what felt like an age ago. "*Things and stuff* ..." I said.

Scarlet looked confused. "*Things and stuff*?"

"Yes. Things and stuff. When the man in the small house saw my sigil, he said he thought it might be a *thing* ... a *thing* that would hide ... *stuff*."

Em rolled her eyes. "Another riddle."

I repeated the Prime Spell Book's words to myself and looked at my friends. "If the sign I hold is the sigil ... and the key is in the air ..." I lifted the necklace over my head and held the sigil in my hand. "Stand back. I'm not sure what this will do." My wand flicked from my sleeve. I removed the crossover potion the Royal Artist had given me from its box and placed a single drop on the end of my wand. "Here goes."

I lifted my wand in the air and traced every line and curve of the sigil, starting at the top and working my way to the bottom. Scarlet, Amber and Em stood back together – their hands clasped in anticipation. Jasper stood at my side.

I finished the last curve and waited. "Nothing," I said.

Amber held her hands up in defeat. "Oh, well. It was worth a try, Daisy."

Scarlet pressed her lips together in disappointment. "Well, tea usually fixes everything," she offered. "Why don't I put the kettle on, and we can see if we can figure this out?"

We reluctantly agreed as Amber held the library door open and we filed out behind Scarlet. She turned to close the door but instead said, "Wait ... Daisy. What is that?"

When we stepped back into the library, a bright apple-green door had appeared right in the middle of the room, its edges bordered with light purple, flowering wisteria. The five of us began encircling the door, being careful not to touch it.

"A door that doesn't lead anywhere ..." Em said curiously. "I'd be careful with that."

"Where do you think it goes?" Amber asked.

Scarlet lifted her hands in the air, tracing the shape of the flowers. "I've never seen anything like it."

"Nor have I," I said. "But there must be a reason the Prime Spell Book brought it here." I reached for its intricately patterned brass handle. "Jasper, do you—"

But before I could utter another word, *the world behind ... was no longer there*.

CHAPTER THIRTY-ONE

A S I HEARD THE soft click of the apple-green door behind me, I felt the coolness of the breeze that followed. I couldn't see much at all. Maybe my eyes were adjusting, but everything was a blur. I rubbed my eyes to adjust to the light, when a voice came from somewhere within the softly lit landscape. I could make out a small figure standing in front of a house – a cottage, from what I could tell. Slowly, the blurred landscape became clearer, and the voice repeated itself, "Daisy ... over here ..."

"Hello," I said back as I took a step forward.

The figure waved a small towel of some sort above their head and started walking towards me.

"It is you!" the voice shouted, before the figure – now clearly a woman – hitched up the sides of her skirt and began running towards me. "I knew you would do it! I just knew it!" she repeated.

As the figure continued to come into focus, there was no denying it. I had seen that face so many times before ... in the portrait hanging in the library.

"Aunt ... Olivia?" I said, as she came to a stop in front of me.

"The one and only," she said with a slight curtsy.

"Where are we?" I asked.

"Well ... in the shadows, of course," she replied as she linked her arm through mine and started walking back towards her cottage. "What do you think? Beautiful, isn't it?"

"I have to say, it's not as dark as I imagined."

"Ah, I thought the same too when I first saw it. The shadows always remain in twilight – we live by candles and crackling fires. It's the place we can finally put our magic to rest. There's no need for it here. It is a magical place all in itself."

She stopped us in front of a small wooden bench: each part made from perfectly worn logs which weaved themselves around the back for a comfortable place to rest. The bench faced away from the cottage, allowing a view deep into the fir tree woods that covered the rolling hillsides of the shadows.

We sat down, and Aunt Olivia took my hand. She was a petite woman with a softened face: a few lines, as anyone would expect for someone of her age, and rose cheeks, indicative of someone with easy access to fresh country air. "I knew you would do it, Daisy. From the moment I laid eyes on you. That fiery red hair ... and those eyes ... There was no doubting it ... you were a Banks witch."

"Well, it has been quite the adventure so far, I must say."

"There is so much more to come for you, Daisy. A little adventure is just the beginning. But I didn't know if this was the life you wanted. And I respected your father's reasoning, so I left strict instructions with Thomas. And if you chose not to stay in Folly Gate, then I had to be sure the secrets the Banks witches kept were taken with me – to the grave. But we will have time to talk about all that later. Right now, I understand you are having problems in the follies, and I may be able to help you. But you will have to do something in return."

"You sound awfully similar to an alchemist I know."

"Morton?"

"Yes."

"You need to work with him," she said without hesitation.

"I do?"

"He was helping me collect the crossover potions."

"So, you do know about the crossover potions?" I asked.

Aunt Olivia tossed her luminous red hair behind her shoulders. "I may have made a crossover potion or two in my time. But I didn't mean for the recipe to be stolen. I have no idea who took it. I thought the recipe would be safe in the Prime Spell Book. But someone knew what they were doing and stole three of the pages. I gave pages to Scarlet and Amber and Em, so that whoever took the pages would never be able to use the most powerful magic that the Prime Spell Book is capable of collecting and dispensing. But crossover potions started appearing ... and none of them had the correct ingredients."

"How did you get the recipe in the first place?" I asked her.

"That may have to be a story for another time, but in short ... the Artist. I don't know how much time you have here, so we have to get straight to the point. The follies: they are alive with adventure. But they are always changing and impossible to map. I thought if I could make a potion that would allow other witches to move easily through the follies, they might be able to help ... but I was wrong ... *so wrong*." She stood up, not letting go of my hand. "Come and see my cottage. I have something to show you."

We walked together along a neat granite cobblestoned path. I looked back to take in the view but couldn't make out any roads or other houses, only woods for as far as the eye could see. Aunt Olivia's cottage sat nestled into the trees; dim light emanated from the front sliding sash windows. Soft plumes of smoke from her chimney rose high above the wildflowers which grew in abundance, and an occasional *buzz-buzzing* could be heard as we continued up the path. I tried to keep quiet and listen to everything she was telling me, but I had so many questions.

"Jasper wasn't to know," she continued. "He may be a cat ... but he is a Banks through and through. It is my advice that you always stick together in the follies, and, if we had more time, I could tell you about all the adventures Jasper and I have had together. However, as time goes on, Jasper will lose memories of us together – they will fade. Never completely, but the old memories will fill with fresh memories ... memories of *your* life with him. It's hard enough to remember everything someone does in one lifetime, but with the amount of lives a cat has, I imagine it would be almost impossible. I suppose it's a mercy, really. In Jasper's earnest trying to get the crossover potion to Gwendolyn as quickly as he could, he didn't know the map had changed. You must always carry your maps with you in the follies. And as it is only the Banks witches that know how to read the maps, we are the only ones allowed to use them without permission. Gwendolyn will ask you before she grants permission to *anyone* – so you can check the map and give current directions to whoever is going into the follies."

"But what can we do about the follies collapsing? There are bats flying around with a crossover potion, and they could be anywhere."

"Well, I may know where you can start fixing that problem at least."

Aunt Olivia opened the cottage door. It was as warm as it looked and welcomed me with the same feelings that greeted me in Ailsa's potion room. A young woman was lifting an old-fashioned kettle off the hob, its handle neatly wrapped in a red and white chequered cloth.

"Tea?" she asked without turning around.

"I'm not sure we have time for it," Aunt Olivia said.

The young woman turned and placed the kettle on a small tile on the kitchen table.

Aunt Olivia introduced us, "Skye, this is my niece Daisy. She's going to help you out of your ... *predicament.*"

"She is?" The young woman stepped over to me and wrapped her arms around me. "Oh, thank you," Skye said. "What a mess I've made of things. I'm so sorry. I won't do anything like this ever again. I promise."

"Anything like what?" I asked.

Aunt Olivia grabbed a teacup and poured herself a tea. "You two won't have time for tea," she said, turning to look out of the window as if to check for something. "Daisy ... Skye is the reason the follies are collapsing."

"She is?"

I looked at the nervous young witch that stood before me and wondered how someone so timid and innocent looking could cause so much damage.

Aunt Olivia sipped her tea. "Sometimes experimenting with magic above your level doesn't end so well. You need to take her back, Daisy ... while you still can."

"Well, how do I do that?"

"Easily ... the same way you came in: through the apple-green door."

"Are you coming, too?" I asked.

"Oh, no. It's too late for me. It is time for me to rest in the shadows. But Skye, well, she is *trapped,* and if you hadn't arrived in the next week or so, she might have ended up resting here too – forever. But it's not her time, and I was sure you would figure it out somehow. Crossover potions are very dangerous, Daisy. You can become trapped in the shadows far earlier than you should. And if no one arrives within one lunar cycle, you are destined to rest." She looked out of her window again and took another sip of tea. "Ah, the apple-green door has returned. You have to leave. Take Skye with you and you'll have to figure out the rest ... You have a lot of loyal witches surrounding you, Daisy. You'll never find more devoted sisters in the craft than Ailsa and Edlynn. Tell them I'm resting well."

"But what about—" I started.

Aunt Olivia embraced me. "We will speak the next time the shadows allow. Take this." She pressed a small stone into my hand. "You'll know when to use it when you need to know it. We are all here, Daisy – as far back as the Banks' line goes. Oh, and one more thing. Take care of our Jasper. We miss him terribly."

CHAPTER THIRTY-TWO

I WOKE TO AILSA'S voice, my head resting against her and cradled in her hand.

"Daisy. You're all right," she whispered.

I turned my head to see Scarlet helping to lift Skye up onto her elbows. We were back in the library and there was no sign of the apple-green door.

"Are you okay, Skye?" I asked.

"I think so," she said as she sat up.

"Edlynn's on her way," Ailsa said as she helped me to my feet.

"I saw her ..." I said.

"Saw who?" Ailsa asked as she removed a loose strand of hair from my face and tucked it behind my ear.

"Aunt Olivia ... she said to tell you she is resting well," I answered.

"Olivia?" Em shook her head. "You went to the shadows? I told you that door was trouble."

"There was no trouble," I said. "It was rather beautiful, in fact, in its own way."

Amber stepped towards Skye. "Well, you've brought something back with you. I hope you know what you're doing."

"I'm not entirely sure," I admitted. "But Aunt Olivia said we will figure out the rest."

Edlynn's voice interrupted us as it carried through from the kitchen, "Is she back yet?" she yelled as she skidded into the library. "Oh, thank goodness," she said when she saw me with Ailsa.

But Edlynn was not alone. Tiggy was behind her, carrying a small transparent red box. Ailsa's shoulders stiffened as she stepped back from me. Tiggy stopped and looked at Ailsa before slowly walking towards me, her boots on the wooden floor cracking through the silence. She passed me the box.

"I found this box," Tiggy said. "It could be an alchemist's tool. And I have a friend who says they might know where there are more."

Ailsa stood in silence as Tiggy agreed to bring any more boxes she might find to me, whilst Edlynn looked at them both hopefully. Everyone in the room kept quiet, like they were waiting for someone to draw their wand.

Ailsa cleared her throat.

"I brought something for you too, Ailsa." Tiggy held up a small, ribboned box.

"I can only imagine where it has come from," Ailsa said defiantly.

"My kitchen, Ailsa," Tiggy replied. "My kitchen ..." – she drew in a breath – "I made you these."

Ailsa strained over to see the package as Tiggy undid the blue ribbon tied around the gift box.

"Butterscotch," Tiggy said as she pushed the opened box towards her. "Just try one, Ailsa."

Ailsa's shoulders softened as she reached for the box. "You know I can never say no to butterscotch."

Tiggy passed her the box and held her arms out as Ailsa took a tentative step towards her. "Please Ailsa," Tiggy pleaded. "Hasn't this gone on long enough? I can't bear another moon without my sister."

Ailsa looked at her sister. "Well ... I suppose you're right. And I also suppose the butterscotch is a good start."

Tiggy pulled her sister in and embraced her.

"All right, all right," Ailsa said. "Be careful. You'll crack a rib, Tiggy."

Edlynn clasped her hands together in delight.

"How did you get here so quickly?" Ailsa asked. But Tiggy's face was not showing the answer Ailsa was looking for. "I knew it!" Ailsa said angrily as she stepped back from her sister.

Tiggy defended herself, "It's not what you think, Ailsa. I promise. Here, let me show you."

Tiggy left the library, returning with a broomstick in her hand. "You see this handle, Ailsa? *Carved* ... by my own hands. Just the way you taught me. And the willow used ... collected from my own garden."

Ailsa looked over the broomstick. "You made this?"

"With my own two hands, Ailsa."

Edlynn stood next to Ailsa. "Tiggy, did you craft the broomstick I used last night?"

"Yes, Edlynn," she replied. "I've been working day and night on them, but didn't think anyone would be interested in something I made. So, I created a story about having to get them from a trader – one that no one knew anything about."

"Well," Ailsa said. "If you did indeed make this broomstick, Tiggy ... you should be proud of yourself. Exquisite craftsmanship."

Tiggy let out a breath. "Oh, thank you, Ailsa. I really am proud of myself."

"Well, I'm glad that's sorted out," Em interjected dismissively. "But is no one going to mention what you brought back from the shadows?"

We turned our attention to Skye.

"Well, it looks like you found our rogue witch, Daisy," Edlynn said. "Maybe Dawn did in fact get the only sour cherry in your cake, after all."

"Maybe she did," I said. "But perhaps we should keep that to ourselves. I feel bad enough about suspecting she might be a rogue witch. I wouldn't want her knowing we thought she was, when nothing could be further from the truth. But yes, I think we have found our rogue witch."

Skye looked across the library at me. "I'm sorry. I'm *so* sorry. I've said I will never do anything like that again. Here ..." She reached into her skirt pocket and passed me a small red potion bottle. "I want nothing to do with crossover potions again ... *ever*."

A whoosh of air filled the library.

"*Gwendolyn* ..." I said under my breath.

The High Priestess appeared at the library door in her usual fashion. However, this time, there was someone standing next to her.

"Lucinda!" I exclaimed as we all drew our wands.

We all stood poised for strike, everyone but Skye.

"Lower your wands, witches," Gwendolyn commanded. "It seems we have some matters to discuss."

❦❦❦❦❦ ❦❦❦❦❦

Lucinda held a spell book in her hands. "I'm giving this to you, Daisy – for safekeeping. And I hope you will understand I was only trying to save my sister." She looked across at Skye. "We're going to be taught under Gwendolyn," she said. "No more practicing on our own."

"We are?" Skye asked.

I took the spell book from Lucinda and placed it on the table next to the now closed Prime Spell Book. "Sisters?" I asked.

Gwendolyn answered, "Yes. Sisters. And sisters with the potential to be very good witches. But they must learn the basics ... the foundations of magic. Which brings me to you, Ailsa."

"Me?" Ailsa asked, not hiding her surprise.

"Yes," Gwendolyn continued. "You will take them under your tutelage."

"Of course, High Priestess," she answered.

"Oooh, a personal recommendation from the High Priestess," I heard Tiggy whisper to Ailsa as she squeezed her arm.

"You'll need these," Gwendolyn said as she passed Ailsa a scroll. "Instructions and registration for your new students. And there is also one other matter," – she passed Ailsa another scroll – "this one confirms your promotion to Master Potion Maker of the Southern Covens."

"A master?" Ailsa asked. "But that means ..."

"That's right ..." Gwendolyn confirmed. "For your commitment to the old ways ... a *new* line of witches. The Grand Coven has been informed and unreservedly agrees."

Tiggy turned to her sister and hugged her so hard Ailsa spluttered before turning back to her friends proudly.

Edlynn ran to her friend. "Merry Meet, Ailsa and Tiggy of the Dawes line."

Ailsa smiled with tears in her eyes. "Merry Meet, my friend Edlynn, of the Cottle line."

"And there's one more thing before I leave," Gwendolyn said as we all turned to her. "Well, two, in fact." Gwendolyn shot her arm towards the library door. A tall black hat, with its pointed top glistening in the candlelight, floated straight over to me.

"A hat?" I asked.

"You've done more than enough to deserve it, Daisy. The Southern Covens are *proud* of their shadow witches." She reached into her robe.

"*And*, as agreed with Morton, the map." She passed me a large rolled-up and corner-worn map, before holding her hand out to me. Without hesitation, I handed her the crossover potion Skye had given me. Gwendolyn smiled. "Maybe alchemists are our friends … after all."

Skye stepped forward. "High Priestess. Before we go. My bat … I think he is still trapped in the follies."

Gwendolyn glided towards her. "I think you'll find that he is now a *cauldron* of bats."

"A *cauldron*?" Skye asked.

"A *cauldron* … a group of bats." Gwendolyn replied.

"Thank you, High Priestess. But I know what a cauldron of bats—"

"Good," Gwendolyn interrupted.

"I'm sorry, Skye," Lucinda said. "I used a multiplicity spell, hoping they would have a better chance of finding you. But when I made it out of the follies, they were nowhere to be seen."

"I have a potion for reversing multiplicity spells," Ailsa offered proudly.

"Good," Gwendolyn said as she scanned the room.

"And I can take Amber and Em to look for Skye's bat," Scarlet offered. "With your permission, of course, High Priestess."

Gwendolyn looked across at me. I breathed in and gave a gentle nod.

"Granted," Gwendolyn said. "Now, I think that is all for now. Enjoy your celebrations and *Merry Pass*, witches." And in a whoosh of air, she disappeared, with Lucinda and Skye following behind her.

CHAPTER THIRTY-THREE

J ASPER STOOD AT MY side as I shared my visit to the shadows with my coven, Tiggy and attached shadow witches – Scarlet, Amber and Em.

"Did Olivia say when you can go back?" Amber asked.

I shrugged my shoulders lightly. "She only said when the shadows allow ... whatever that means. But I have a feeling it has something to do with lunar cycles. She did, however, give me this before I left."

I held the small grey stone up to them in my open palm. It showed a silver sigil engraved into it.

"Haven't we been here before?" Em asked with a tinge of sarcasm.

"We have," I replied calmly. "She said I would know when to use it."

"When do you think that might be?" Scarlet asked.

"Well ... now," I said as I flicked my wand from my sleeve. "Let's see what it does."

I traced the sigil in the air with my wand as I had done before visiting the shadows.

"Look," Edlynn said. "The Prime Spell Book ..."

My wand snapped back into my sleeve. Both the Prime Spell Book and Lucinda's spell book were open, and a luminous magenta stream of words and shapes and symbols were passing in the air, back and forth between them.

"It's collecting the spells," Ailsa said in a hushed tone. "I had heard they could do that, but I've never seen it."

"It's beautiful," Amber said. "Can you imagine what other spells it may have hidden in there?"

"Who knows?" Edlynn said. "It could have been doing this for centuries."

"It's up to us to figure it out," I said as we watched the magenta light begin to fade. "Well, that must be it. We'll collect as many spell books as we can and return the Prime Spell Book back to its most powerful."

The Prime Spell Book slammed shut. I picked up Lucinda's spell book and squeezed it into a space on the bookshelf next to my aunt's reading chair.

"Well," Scarlet began, "I think we better find this bat so that we can head home tomorrow."

"I'll take you to my potion room," Ailsa said. "And Tiggy ... we have a lot of catching up to do."

"I'll see you all out," Edlynn said. "I think Daisy could use a good sleep."

"Without a doubt, Edlynn," I said as I flopped into my aunt's chair. Jasper joined me at my feet. "Merry Pass, witches."

"Merry Meet again," they replied in unison.

"You've done well, my witch," Jasper purred.

"Thank you, Jasper. I think we need a well-deserved break."

Edlynn returned to the library. "Is there anything I can get you before I go?"

"There is one thing ... and I don't know that I'll sleep before looking ..."

"What's that?"

"Morton's map ..."

"Well, surely that can wait. You must be exhausted."

"It will only take a minute."

"Go on then. There doesn't seem to be any stopping you."

I smiled and unrolled the map out onto the desk, holding the corners down with glass flower paperweights.

"Unsurprisingly blank," Edlynn said.

"It's not blank, Edlynn. But I don't recognise ... It looks like somewhere in Spain. *La Cueva de las Brujas* ..."

"*La Cueva de las Brujas*," Edlynn repeated. "The Cave of the Witches."

"You speak Spanish?"

"I took a class ... a long time ago. A folly that takes us to Spain? Well, it looks like someone thinks we need a holiday, Daisy. Pack your bags. We're off to Spain!"

"It looks like we are," I said excitedly.

"But first, Daisy ... you need some rest. Take this." She handed me a small dark bottle.

"Oh, no thanks," I said. "I think I've had enough of potions for a bit."

"It's not a potion, Daisy ... *technically*. English Lavender – a few drops on your pillow. Upstairs you go. We'll take care of everything while you sleep."

"Thanks, Edlynn. The last few days have been quite chaotic."

Jasper followed me up the stairs. I kicked off my boots at the door. "A few drops ..." I said before laying my head down on the soft pillow and filling my dreams with *Spain* ... and *spells* ... and *sangria* ...

※ ※ ※

I sipped my tea, after a long uninterrupted sleep, and admired my sitting room.

"They might have overdone it," Jasper said before releasing a small sneeze.

"I think they're beautiful," I said.

My three houseguests had left me with a room covered in enormous vases, filled with wildflowers of every colour. A note left on my coffee table read:

'Merry Meet again, Daisy,
We didn't want to wake you. All is well.
Blessed Be,
Scarlet, Amber and Em'

"A quiet house again, Jasper," I said. "I think I might even miss them a little."

Jasper purred.

"Well, what do you think about some fresh mackerel for lunch?" I asked him.

"I would never say no, my witch," he replied politely.

"Good. Give me a minute and we'll head off."

After a quick change of clothes, we walked into town, stopping in at Carter's for Jasper's lunch and picking up some lunch for me. We walked out of Home Sweet Scone and headed down the High Street towards the town green. I would have walked straight past Jenifer's bookshop, if not for the fact she was dressing her window and we caught her eye. She stepped down and came to the front of the shop.

"Changing things up," she said. "I completely sold out of *In a Manor of Steeping*."

I let out a slight groan that was louder than intended.

"Something the matter?" Jenifer asked with a raised eyebrow. "I would have thought you would be pleased."

"Under normal circumstances, I most certainly would. But *In a Manor of Steeping* received such terrible reviews ..."

"It did?" She tilted her head to the side. "I had no idea."

I paused for a moment in an awkward silence. I wasn't sure I believed her.

Jenifer continued, "Well, maybe next time I'll display *Criss Cross Croissant* instead."

"It's not that I'm ungrateful ..." I continued.

"Of course, you're not," Jenifer said, as she locked her eyes with mine.

"Okay," I said, holding onto my suspicions. "Thank you."

"You're welcome, Daisy. Anything to help support local business. Well, I better get back to it," she said, and turned on her booted heel back into her shop.

I continued down the High Street with Jasper, passing the Market Square being prepared for the upcoming festival. A small team worked on building a stage that tomorrow would fill with live music, and stalls that would fill with fresh farm produce and preserves, and with trinkets, jewellery and artwork from local craft makers.

I looked down at Jasper. "I think Jenifer knew exactly what she was doing," I said.

"She did sound like she knew which of your books was a bestseller."

"Well, I'll have to keep my eye on her," I said. "But for now, let's enjoy our lunch. How about the bench next to the sweet chestnut tree?"

I unwrapped the mackerel-filled paper parcel from Carter's fishmongers and set it on the ground for Jasper, before opening my lunch on the bench, next to me. I was about to take a bite when I saw Ethan's car pull up on the side of the street. He got out and gave me a wave.

"Looks like you've been to Home Sweet Scone, too," I said as he approached.

"Baxter is a master," he joked. "Do you mind if I join you for lunch? I was going to eat it in the car," – he looked around – "but I saw you ... and—"

"Of course," I said. "I haven't seen you for a couple of days. You can catch me up on what's been happening with Amie."

"Amie ... well, she's going to be away for a long time, especially as we are adding fraud charges, too. We found a copy of a forged will in her suitcase. It looks like Amie was planning to take everything from Kate and Ellie. However, she came unstuck when she used an outdated template from a London solicitor. Amie must have been planning this for quite a while. The rest of Kate and Ellie's trust was to be released on Kate's thirtieth birthday. But little did Amie know that the only solicitor everyone in Folly Gate protects their estates with is ..."

"Thomas Cartwright," we said together.

"Right," Ethan said. "A quick phone call to him and he was able to give me a copy of Kate's updated will."

"How awful. And the captain?"

"I visited Mrs Gabris and her daughter. They are never easy visits to make."

"I'm sure."

"Daisy ... if you hadn't arrived at Kate's house when you did—"

I gave him a friendly pat on the knee. "It's okay," I said with a smile. "Eat your lunch."

"Well, Home Sweet Scone do make the best sandwiches." Ethan inspected his roll before taking a large bite. "I think it's that hand-rolled butter with the flakes of salt."

"You might be right," I said as I took a bite of mine.

Ethan looked across at my filled roll. "No roast beef for you today?"

"Seafood salad ..." I replied.

"A little exotic for you, Dais', wouldn't you say?"

Jasper lifted his head from his mackerel and looked up at us.

"Not today, Ethan," I said with a grin. "*Today*, as it happens, I'm feeling a little adventurous."

Afterword

Thank you for joining Daisy and Jasper on another adventure in Folly Gate.

If you enjoyed spending time with them, please consider leaving an honest review on the platform you purchased this book from. As an independent author, reviews are an important part of keeping this series successful. I appreciate any feedback, and it helps other paranormal cosy mystery fans find my books and know what you thought about them. Every single review makes a difference and helps me continue doing what I love, which is to bring more adventures with Daisy, Jasper and their friends to you. Thank you for spending time with them and I hope to see you again soon!

Luna

Want to keep updated about Luna's releases?
Visit: www.lunamartin.com

YOU CAN ALSO FOLLOW LUNA ON SOCIAL
MEDIA
FACEBOOK: www.facebook.com/lunamartinauthor

About Author

Luna lives in Devon, UK, where mysteries are a large part of county history. When she is not writing, she enjoys walks with her husband and much-loved dog throughout the Devonshire, Cornish and Welsh countryside. She also loves baking bread and delicious cakes, spending time in the garden and anything else that makes a house a home.

Potions and Prosecco is her second novel in the Merry Meet Cozy Witch Mysteries Series.

COMING SOON

Spells and Sangria: Merry Meet Cozy Witch Mysteries – Book 3

Printed in Great Britain
by Amazon

25877166R00148